Three Blue Candles

This is the first novel by Dr. David E. McNamara. He is the
author of the non-fiction book
The Exemplary Teacher, published by Neason Hill Press in
2010

This imprint is set in the typeface font Osaka, a delightful and
easy to read style.

Three Blue Candles

David Edward McNamara

Neason Hill Press

Three Blue Candles. Copyright 2011 by Dr. David Edward McNamara, All Rights Reserved. Printed in the United States of America. For information, contact Neason Hill Press.

Library of Congress Cataloging-in-Publication Data
McNamara, David, Edward, Dr., 1956-
Three Blue Candles: a novel/ David E. McNamara, MD., 1st ed.
ISBN 978-0-9826982-1-1
First Edition: October 2011
10 9 8 7 6 5 4 3 2 1

Dedication

This work of fiction is dedicated to all of the brave men and women who have returned from war zones having been traumatized and are fighting for recovery. It is dedicated to individuals who suffer the after effects of a trauma in their lives. Whether they are recognized to have PSTD or not their paths to recovery are similar. A portion of the proceeds from the sales of this book will be donated to the Wounded Warrior Project.

Prologue

It was more of a resuscitation than a delivery. She lay in the birthing bed cold and incoherent. She yelped loudly and looked frightened.

"She says her due date is Christmas, so she is a week early. That's all we could get out of her." The medical student briefed the obstetrician as they entered the doctor's lounge. The young doctor in training continued.

"Someone found her in an alley near Mary Herman College. She was moaning and quite cold."

The senior doctor looked at him as he put his Rolex on the night stand and grabbed some blue scrubs. His skin was pale and baggy. The medical student studied him as he changed.

"How many years do I have to be on staff at this place before I don't need to drive in here on a cold December night for a welfare case." He continued while washing his hands, his face in a contorted scowl. "How far along is she?"

"We don't know. There is no record of any prenatal care that I can find. And I think she must be high on drugs or something but she isn't talking." He raised his hands in the air for emphasis and continued. "She's fully dilated and 100% effaced. The nurses already have her pushing."

"OK, then let's go have a delivery. No prenatal care, all kinds of medical and psychiatric issues, Mother of God, why me? These are the ones who usually end up in a lawsuit."

The student followed his mentor into the birthing room and they said their hellos. The patient lay on the table with her legs askew. She had a warming blanket over her and the anesthesiologist struggled to get an intravenous started. Her eyes looked away like a pope's in a procession. As the contractions came she awoke from her stupor, moaned, and pushed. The room was lit with florescent lights. It had nice window treatments, silk flowers, and pastel colors. Despite the hospital's efforts to make it look familiar, it had an institutional aura.

The charge nurse whispered to the doctor outside the door as the two looked in. "I know most of the pregnant girls in Erie, but I am not sure who this is. Her drug screen is positive for opiates and cocaine. Her thighs are quite bruised. She has been living on the street and she is quite hypothermic."

The Ob-Gyn gathered his thoughts then entered and turned to the young girl introducing himself. He extended his hand warmly.

"OK, So now we are going to have a baby." he said in his most feigned cheerful voice.

She looked at him for a long time and then smiled ever so slightly. Soon the neonatal team entered sleepily with their brightly lit glass incubator and tiny stethoscopes. Everybody was prepared for a difficult birth and a compromised newborn.

When the baby arrived it was a boy and he was quite robust. He cried loudly and was wiped dry. The mother sighed and spoke loudly surprising everyone in the room.

"I want to see him. Is he OK? I want to hold him. Please hand him to me doctor."

The doctor placed the newborn in the delivering mom's arms. She looked him in the eyes and appeared frightened. She knew those eyes. They were partly the reflection of her own but they were his eyes as well. She tried not to look away. She could feel anxiety coming quickly like a summer storm. The nurse took the newborn from her and handed him to the pediatricians. The new mom was wheeled to a quiet room.

In the morning snow was piling up on the window ledge outside. She could see the white clouds moving across the sky from her bed. She heard footsteps and muffled conversation outside her room. Social services arrived with a judge's determination that her baby would be taken into the state's custody. They brought the nurse to her bedside and tried to be very nice about it. She was lonely again and felt a deep ache inside that had nothing to do with the delivery. She waited quietly for the nurses to discharge her to the streets.

Chapter 1

Arnold Minor Benson paced nervously in front of the class rubbing his head. The professor was an elderly man with kindly eyes, grey hair that seemed to emanate from one area of his scalp, and a nervous energy. You could see it just before he was about to speak. A motion in his face that wasn't a tick but rather as if a mallard was frightened in the water. That momentary thrust backward and more erect, with wings and legs and water splashing, then almost remarkably, airborne.

"All happy families resemble one another, each unhappy family is unhappy in its own way."

A number of hands shot up. He pointed to a young man in a polo shirt.

"Leo Tolstoy. Anne Karenia."

"Almost perfect. Anna Karenia. Anna. You should know Anna."

"Yes Anna."

"Good.

The professor paced. Winter sunlight streaked across the classroom and brightened the wooden floor. It would be his last year at Mary Herman College. He was retiring after spring semester, in a few months. He had loved his years in the English Department and his classes had grown bigger and more popular. But after thirty-eight years sharing creative writing skills he wanted to travel and spend more time with his grandkids.

The professor muttered. "When sorrows come they come not single spies, but battalions..."

Hands went up throughout the hall. The professor looked around and smiled.

"Maybe you are learning something. Maybe things have gotten too easy for you." He turned to Nicki, a well liked junior.

"OK. You can tell us what you know."

"Shakespeare's Hamlet. King Claudius is speaking to Gertrude."

"Yes, Yes, Yes. Of course." The professor removed his tortoise-shell glasses, rubbed his eyes, and continued. "And why do I focus on these two quotes, out of the many I could have suggested?" He paused rhetorically, and like the mallard flying high with the wings of lawn ornament he answered his own question. "Because I want your creative writing projects to get at the unhappy endings, the sorrows, the truth, and the feelings that are the real part of our lives."

The class followed him as he moved across the front of the room. His pace quickened and he turned to the students almost as an explosion, glasses crooked, hair disheveled. And then he spoke.

"Happy stories are boring stories. Please remember that if you remember anything. Class dismissed."

Arnold Minor Benson closed his soft briefcase and the students stood and started to exit. Conversational laughter bounced off the wooden walls. Nicki and Emily linked at the north exit and headed up the path toward the student apartments. It was a cold February Friday, and although the forecast called for more snow, it didn't appear that the weather was threatening. Their feet made a crunching sound as they moved along the frozen path.

They were roommates from freshman year and acted like sisters. When Emily competed in cross country or played piano recitals Nicki was there. When Nicki ran for student counsel Emily campaigned as her manager. Neither kept a secret from the other. Over Christmas break Emily spent time with Nicki's family in Harrisburg.

"I have to go to Student Health this afternoon to get my pills refilled."

"Oh Nicki, that sounds like fun."

Nicki laughed. "Actually I'm kind of dreading it. Will you go with me?"

Emily looked at her watch. "I was planning to go for a run. I missed the team run yesterday and I need to train. Do you really need me?"

Nicki smiled. "No. I'll be OK. Do you want to hook up later."

"Yes, definitely. I thought we could go over to the mall. I need a blouse for tonight's Hockey party."

"OK. I would love that."

Nicki turned to Emily and put her arm on her shoulder. "By the way I was talking to some of the varsity guys and they made a point of stressing that I ask you to come to the party."

Emily smiled widely and her eyes twinkled. She was tickled that some players would ask for her by name.

"That is so nice, but you know that I volunteer at the Erie City Mission on Friday evenings."

"Yeah but you could stop by on your way home."

Emily smiled again.

"OK, Maybe. I'll catch you later, Nicki."

"Text me."

"Good luck with the doctor."

The girls split on different paths. In the middle distance and low in the western sky one small dark cloud appeared. Maybe a storm is coming after all, Emily whispered to herself.

Chapter 2

Emily Verada changed into her black cold weather tights and slipped a turtleneck over her head. She had strong runner's legs and a sharp figure. Her stomach was flat and her skin clear. She pulled back her shiny blonde hair and clipped it in place. In her pack she placed her fleece headband, gloves, and windbreaker. She grabbed her Ipod Shuffle and her last Powerbar, sat on the end of her bed and slipped on her almost new Asics running shoes. Before leaving she looked across her room, viewed her reflection in the mirror, and smiled softly.

Her yellow VW beetle felt stiff and cold as she turned the key. It struggled to start and then idled rapidly as she put on the wiper and washer to clear the snow off the front window. She cleared the back window with her scraper revealing her Mary Herman University sticker. Underway the warmth came and the remaining window ice started to melt so she felt safe to turn on the music. The route was familiar and within fifteen minutes she was riding down the hill and entering Price Island State Park. The park was one of her favorite running places with miles of paved trails that were kept clear for visitors during the winter months. She pulled into the first parking lot along the Price Island Bay and parked in her usual spot. The bay was frozen and a few fisherman sat in their ice huts in the distance. As she pulled on her hat, gloves, and Ipod she had a brief uncomfortable sensation that she ignored and it passed quickly.

Underway Emily ran at a brisk pace and felt strong. She loved how the ice that stuck to the trees was lit brightly by the sun. Her route took her along the bay and in and out of wooded groves. A few more clouds had formed but it didn't seem ready to snow. She monitored her footing to avoid some isolated patches of ice and overall conditions seemed fine. She turned around at her usual spot and feeling strong picked up her pace. Now it seemed that the slight breeze was behind her. As she briskly moved through a stand of Jack Pines she saw a man coming out from the bay side of a densely wooded area. Something about his demeanor seemed out of place for such a beautiful trail through the woods. He was not a fisherman she concluded. They were always carrying something. He didn't appear to be a walker. They never leave the trail. As she moved closer he stepped into her lane. Emily immediately sensed danger and her heart pounded.

With a strained motion the man lunged at her and she felt herself falling to the snow-covered pavement. Emily saw that his right eye was opacified not unlike a dog's she had seen at the shelter. She moved quickly to get up and break free. She was up and she was confident she could outrun him. The ranger station was nearby. There didn't seem time to scream. Emily felt a severe slap to the back of her head. It seemed strange to her that it didn't hurt but as she fell she tasted blood in her mouth. She wasn't able to get her hands out to stop her fall. She felt extremely cold. Then everything went completely dark.

Chapter 3

Nicki finished lunch at the dining hall and stopped at the library to check out a book for her literature class. When she returned to her suite at about 2:00 pm she was surprised that Emily hadn't returned. Nicki thought nothing of it. Maybe Emily had already run, come back, taken a shower and was getting a late lunch. She quickly thumbed a text message and sent it off.

"Emily-I'm@home. Where ru?, Nicki."

When the phone rang she thought it was Emily but it was her friend Justin, who lived across the complex, and wanted to know if Emily was driving to Pittsburgh this weekend, and if so could he ride with her. Nicki explained what she knew and hung up.

At 3:00 p.m. Nicki started calling Emily on her cell phone only to get voicemail. This surprised Nicki because Emily was always responsible with answering her phone and returning her texts. Maybe something came up and Emily got off on her run late. She would answer when she got back Nicki thought. Nicki felt better. She expected to see Emily walk up the path at any minute. She would give her another thirty minutes to return.

At 3:30 Nicki called and texted again and then went downstairs to Marsha Breeden's suite and knocked on the door. Marsha was a senior and unofficial mother hen for the complex. She answered the door in a white bathrobe her damp hair in a bun.

"I can't find Emily. We were supposed to go to the mall."

Marsha looked concerned. For some of the students Marsha wouldn't be surprised if they disappeared for a few hours or even a few days, but for Emily, who she loved like a sister, this was unusual.

"When did you last see her?"

Nicki told her.

"Did she run from the campus or did she take her car?"

Nicki looked surprised. She assumed Emily would run from the dorms but maybe she did take her car. She walked to the sliding glass door by the table and looked out over the parking lot.

"She must of taken her car. I don't see it where she always parks."

By now the snow had started to fall and the day was darkening. Marsha was on the phone with Jenny, the cross-country team captain while she was blasting emails to her long list of friends on campus and around town.

"Ok, Jenny. I appreciate it. If you hear anything let me know."

Nicki paced back and forth as Martha worked her contacts. Martha spoke nervously belying her words.

"I am sure that she is OK. She knows her way around Erie. Emily has a good head on her shoulders."

Nicki queried. "Do you think she got in a car accident or something?"

"No. I think she is OK. I am sure she will be back soon."

Marsha walked into her bedroom, slipped out of her bathrobe and put on the clothes she had arranged on her bed. Nicki followed her in, pushed some things off the chair and sat down.

"I could call the City Mission. She volunteers over there occasionally on Fridays."

"That's a good idea." Marsha said as she combed out her hair.

"Ok. I will see you at the dining hall in about 45 minutes. If we haven't found Emily by then we can call the campus police."

Nicki felt somewhat reassured. "Sounds like a plan. I will see you there."

At Price Island State Park all park activities ceased at sunset. However the Park roads remained open for a few hours before the gates were closed. The rangers made their first sweep at sunset moving through the parking areas alerting visitors that the park was closing. The second sweep came after darkness at which time all parked cars were to be moved. Overnight the small Bobcat plows ran the multipurpose trails clearing snow and the larger plows cleared the main park roads.

When Officer Brian Matsos arrived in Landing One he saw the yellow beetle parked facing the bay. Snow covered the vehicle and it appeared that it had been sitting for some time. He knew it wasn't an ice fisherman's car. They always parked tail in. Occasionally vehicles were left in the park overnight. Cars had dead batteries or mechanical problems. The owner might have hooked up with a romantic interest and left the car for later. Matsos wasn't immediately surprised by the empty car's presence. He angled his Dodge four wheel drive pickup in toward the driver's door and lit his spotlight. Then he walked to the car and with his gloved hand brushed snow off the window and peered inside. A chocolate Powerbar sat on the passenger seat next to a cell phone with a small green light flashing. An open backpack rested on the back seat.

Matsos returned to his truck and began to think out loud.

"Who would leave their cell phone in their car? Did someone walk out onto the ice and fall through? No, it has been cold for weeks and the ice is solid. No one would fall through in February. Was someone hurt on the trail and taken away by ambulance? No, he would have heard about on report or on the radio? Was foul play involved?"

Matsos paused and rubbed his chin. He decided he would quickly finish his sweep and return. If the vehicle was still there he would run the tags. He pulled out and moved quickly into the darkening day.

Chapter 4

Emily drifted from deep unconsciousness to a state of semi-awareness. She felt moisture on the back of her head and on her hand but she did not recognize it as blood. She could not remember the events leading up to her sleeping state. She had a sense of needing to be somewhere but couldn't remember where. She had a feeling of needing to wake up, like in a dream, but she was unable to come out of her fugue.

She lay on a dark scarred vinyl floor in a damp, cold room. It had become nearly totally dim except for a hallway light that partially lit one wall. The color was pale brown like the wall of her grandfather's basement. The small room appeared empty except for a chain that was bolted solidly in the center of the floor. It snaked across the linoleum and was attached to a shackle that was clamped around her right ankle. Emily instinctively kicked at it as one might a duvet on a hot summer night. There was a distant smell of urine, feces, and death, but it was not hers. She was not aware of her nakedness or that she had wet herself. There might have been the sounds of another girl's whispers but Emily did not hear them.

In the darkest corner of the room a brown recluse spider (loxosceles reclusa) rappelled down to look at his new roommate. The brown recluse is also called the violin spider because if one looks closely behind the three pairs of eyes there are markings that resemble a violin. Interestingly, the violin spider can live for up to 6 months without food or water. It finds darkness during the day and comes out at night to hunt for small insects first paralyzing them with its powerful venom. As Emily slowly turned on the floor the spider moved back up into the dark web.

Outside it was snowing steadily now and a light westerly wind was blowing. The temperature had dropped noticeably and the sky was now dark and low. A long freight train passed nearby and the click clack of its metal wheels transitioned into a dull clatter. Beyond the noise of the wheels there was the subtle ringing of a bell and faint flashing red lights that entered Emily's room. First the soft reflected flashing stopped and then the train noise became quieter and distant and soon it was imperceptible.

It wasn't the train noise that brought Emily up into a dream state, nor the sound of a siren far away. It wasn't the cold, hard floor on her hip and back, or the urine on her leg. What brought her up to near wakefulness was the quiet moaning of someone nearby. It persisted until Emily perceived someone nearby needed help. And that was a cue to which she naturally responded.

The familiar dreams began as they always did. These were the dreams that came when Emily fell off her mountain bike in 5th grade and underwent surgery on her fractured elbow. They came again in Junior High School when her parents bitterly divorced. In High School when the grandmother that she loved so much became ill and died in her arms they lasted weeks. And for a brief period in freshman year at Mary Herman College they surfaced before she met Nicki and the others and started to love the place.

In her dream she found herself walking on a busy road before she became lost. The people crowded her and laughed loudly. She was hungry, tired, and confused.   Then she did something she did not like to do. She asked for help. But the people she asked morphed into monsters and demons. Even the policemen, the doctors, and the people with kind faces morphed into threatening creatures. Next Emily tried to run but could not. She gasped for air but it did not come. As the dream passed she felt her heart pounding.

Emily was awake now. The dream had done it. The blood had dried and caked on the back of her head. The urine had dried on her leg and pooled on the floor. She was crying loudly and with determined fear. Tears where dripping down her face and they tasted salty. She looked around in the darkness and could not stop crying.   Outside the snow continued to fall like ash from a fire in the darkness.

Chapter 5

Matsos pulled his white pickup up behind the yellow VW sitting alone in Landing One at Price Island State Park. He radioed in the Pennsylvania tags and waited for a reply.

"2007 VW New Beetle, Color Yellow, registered to Derek and Joanne Verada, of Sewickley, PA. No outstanding warrants." There was a slight squelch in the radio.

"Do you have a contact number?"

"I have a home number for the Sewickley address. I will give it to you and then patch you through."

"Copy, and Thank you."

Joanne Verada, Emily's mother answered the phone. Matsos queried. "Are you the owner of a yellow 07 VW beetle?"

"That's my daughter's car. Is everything alright?"

Matsos identified himself and explained the situation. Joanne thought aloud. "I know Emily runs at Price Island. Did she leave the car to go with friends, maybe to the mall or something?"

"Usually that's how these situations turn out. However, I see a cell phone on the passenger seat of the vehicle."

Joanne sighed audibly. "I don't think she would have left her cell phone like that if she was leaving with friends."

Matsos suspected that something was wrong. It didn't have the feel of a mechanical or a missing person. He was a proud officer and he smelled something he didn't like.

"Ma'am, would you please try to track down your daughter and if you find her would you leave word with the Park Ranger's Office." He gave her the number.

"Yes sir, Thank you."

Matsos pulled out of Landing One and drove slowly along the road that paralleled the trail into the park. He shined his searchlight onto the trail looking for anything suspicious. Seeing nothing out of the ordinary he drove to the shed where the plow operators where getting ready to clear the multipurpose trails. He explained the situation and asked them to be on the lookout for anything that might be helpful.

In Emily and Nicki's suite a small group had gathered to get the word out to try to locate her. Calls were placed to all of the possible places she might be. Did she hook up with an old boyfriend? Was she at the City Mission? Was she hurt and at the hospital? Did her dad come up from Philadelphia. Everything came up empty.

At 6:45 p.m. Joanne Verada called Nicki and it was decided they would call the police. After Nicki got off the phone she turned to the others and spoke.

"Emily's mom is coming up tonight. She wants us to call the police. They found her yellow beetle at Price Island."

There was gasp and then silence. Moments earlier the students had a working optimism that this was some misunderstanding and that Emily would walk through the door with a simple explanation. They would all hug and laugh, a few would have a beer, and all would be well. They would even be able to go to the hockey party as planned. Now the mood was somber.   Nicki walked to the phone without looking at the others and dialed the police.

Joanne dialed her ex-husband and left a voicemail for him to call her. She got together enough things for a few days and loaded the BMW X5.   Before she turned the key she prayed out loud.

"Please dear lord, do not take another child from me?"

On route she called her former spouse again. Next she dialed her sister in Tacoma who tried to downplay the situation and offered any help she could.   When Derek Verada called back from Detroit he explained that oddly he had been in Erie earlier in the day to change planes but that he hadn't seen or heard from her. He offered his help and asked Joanne to keep him posted.

The roads were clear until the I-80 crossing about halfway up and then they became snow-covered for most of the rest of the trip. Despite the conditions there wasn't much traffic and Joanne pushed her pace.   Under the best of circumstances she could make it in about two hours, but even with her anxiety to get to Mary Herman College as quickly as possible it was taking longer that she thought.   Driving by herself and focused on the road she wondered what her Derek was doing in Erie, and why he wouldn't have even tried to contact Emily. She intended to confront him on that but she wanted to bight her tongue and wait until she got to Emily's suite to see if there was any need.

Chapter 6

The man entered the brick building through a rear metal door that was locked with a dead bolt. He walked through a large area where boats of all sizes were stored, some in the process of being painted, others covered tightly in blue plastic shrink wrap. Across the floor in the southwest corner was an engine area where outboard motors were lined up along a row. There was a bench and various tools and engine parts strewn around. It smelled of oil, gasoline, and decaying fish. Down a dimly lit hall from the work area was a service elevator that he entered. It descended one floor to a smaller area that at one time may have been the business offices of the factory. Through a locked door at the end of the hall were three small rooms that may have been used to store cash and valuables in an earlier day. These were the rooms where the man now kept his girls.   There was an additional room in this part of the building, probably once a secretary's area, now being used far differently.

The man entered the secretary's room, switched on the light, and prepared his equipment. He wheeled a wooden box with various attachments out into the hall outside of Emily's room. Now that the hallway was lit Emily could see out the small window of her door. She saw the man and it startled her.

His opacified eye stung deep in her consciousness. Because of her blow to the head and resultant amnesia she could not immediately place him. She sensed he meant her nothing good.

He smiled as he entered the room. His teeth were crooked and yellow. Emily pulled away as far as she could but was limited by the chain and shackle on her right ankle. While Emily was still chained to the floor he placed her on his wooden contraption on her hands and knees with her belly resting on the wooden box. She resisted as much as possible but in a weakened state from fear and injury she was no match for the heavier man. She was shackled at the wrists and forearms and at the knees and finally the ankles. Then the man strapped a long leather belt through cut outs in the box and around Emily's abdomen. Emily pleaded with him to stop and to let her go. She began crying again. The man laughed and wheeled her naked body into the secretary's room.

Down the hall away from Emily's sight were two additional rooms where the other girls where confined, chained to the floor. The first, from northeastern Ohio, had been captured six days earlier and was becoming very weak, having had no food nor water, and undergoing nearly daily abuse. The second girl, from the Jamestown, New York area was taken eleven days earlier and had been quiet for the last two days. It seemed as is the man was now ignoring her.

After a short time the girl in the second room could hear the screams from the secretary's room and the grunting and laughter from the man. She knew exactly what was happening. She knew every detail of it. She lay in her own room chained at the ankle nearly delirious from lack of sustenance but strong enough to wish she could break free to help her. She could not. She prayed for Emily instead.

Outside the snow had nearly stopped and some stars were shining in between the clouds. The wind was still and people were home in their houses. As the air cleared it became quite cold. Snow coated the entire city like a blanket. An airplane moved slowly across the sky without making a sound.

Chapter 7

The campus policeman was the first officer to arrive. He sat at the table in the kitchen and took notes on a small spiral bound notepad. He had a red face and a potted nose. His eyes were pale blue and his hair cropped short and white. He had spent many a friday evening investigating a student prank or helping a drunken coed back to the dorm so he a slight air of nonchalance in his questioning. Nicki let the other girls answer his questions unless she was needed. She was busy texting her football friends to organize a search and rescue for Price Island.

"Yes, at about 11:40 a.m. Her last class ended about twenty minutes earlier."

The officer took notes moving his finger to his mouth before he turned the page.

"Who was the last person to see her?"

The girls pointed to Nicki. Nicki walked to the table.

"Are you her roommate?"

"Yes, and her best friend."

"How tall is she?"

"Five feet seven and a half inches."

"And does she have any distinguishing marks or tattoos?"

Nicki smiled. "No tattoos. She has a scar on her left elbow from an operation to set the bone."

Joanne Verada knocked on the door and let herself in. The officer stood and she introduced herself. She had a winter tan and there was urgency in her face. She spoke to the officer.

"Did the girls tell you they found her car at Price Island?"

"Yes, Mrs Verada. We are filing with the Erie and Millcreek Police as well as the Erie County Sheriff's Office. They will certainly put out a statewide alert. Usually we wait 48 hours on these missing person cases, but I think these circumstances warrant moving forward."

Joanne Verada nodded. She sat at the table. One of the girls brought the elders cups of coffee. Joanne sipped at hers, black.

"Do you have a recent picture of Emily" he asked.

The girls scurried into the bedroom and printed something up. When they returned they placed some pictures on the table and the officer looked at them sipping his coffee.

"Yes, I know who she is now. Isn't she one of the cross country runners?"

The girls nodded.   Joanne spoke.   "Yes, she is on varsity."

The officer pursed his lips, chose a photo, folded it in half and put it in his pocket. He stood with the help of his arms and his face grew slightly more red. He reached into his pocket and handed Joanne his card.

"I will get right on this. Here is the number that we will use to centralize all information. Don't hesitate to check in at anytime."

Joanne nodded. Everyone stood and the red-faced man exited. Joanne took off her long down jacket and hugged Nicki and the others. Texts were coming in from Nicki's friends from across campus offering to help in anyway possible. The question the girl's discussed was whether to ride over to Price Island immediately or wait for the morning.

Chapter 8

The dark and damp room where Emily lay was quiet. There was semen and blood on her leg. She felt a deep ache far inside and she had dry heaves. Since she returned from the secretary's room she cried and then fell into a deep sleep. The sleep produced frightening dreams and then she was awake. Awake and confused.

She asked herself what was actually happening. After all she was a Mary Herman College student. It was a nice school and she was a good student. She didn't deserve to be punished like this. What had she done to be punished like this? She was living in Erie. Erie was a safe city. She had never had any trouble before. She did not have any enemies. Could this be a drug overdose? Was she hallucinating? She did not take drugs she told herself.

She quieted her mind again. But her shallow breathing returned. The anxiety came in waves. It overwhelmed her. She felt the room spinning. Her heart was pounding. She tried to pull her leg away but the chain rattled and it grabbed. Maybe it is all a terrible dream she told herself. Yes, maybe I got in a car accident and they are operating on me right now. I am feeling the effects of the anesthesia but as soon as it wears off I will be OK. Yes that must be it. I have heard that anesthesia can produce vivid dreams. She reached to her face to pull the anesthesia mask away. She reached to her arm to pull out her intravenous. There was no mask to remove. There was no intravenous to disconnect.

She tried to calm herself again. She put her right hand on her chest over her heart and felt it pulsing. She held it there. Yes, I am alive she told herself. I am alive. When the surgery is over and the anesthesia wears off I will wake from this terrible dream. But I will have to thank the doctors for taking such good care of me. And I will have to be a more careful driver.

For a little while she fell into a hopeful sleep. The blood had caked in her hair and dried on her leg. She was covered in urine and vomit and purple colored bruises that bloomed on her forearms and lower legs, especially near where she was shackled to the floor. Soon the surgery would be over, she whispered to herself, and the anesthesia would wear off and everything would be OK.

Chapter 9

Joanne and the girls piled into her BMW and headed toward Price Island State Park. They had loaded the hatch with flashlights and Nicki brought the spare set of VW keys that Emily had given her. Nicki sat in the front seat and directed Ms. Verada through the city and down the hill to the park entrance. A steel tubular gate sat across the road with the sign "Park Closed" clearly marked. Joanne pulled to the right side of the road and onto the snow covered shoulder.

The girls walked on the multi-purpose trail for about a half mile until they came to Landing One. There alone sat Emily's beetle. It was covered with snow. The sky was clearer now and there was a half moon that shone in a line across the frozen bay. Across the view the girls saw the lit windows of the houses on the cliff and further along the night skyline of the city of Erie. The city appeared to twinkle in the darkness. Nicki opened the car and grabbed Emily's cell phone. She put it in her pocket. After she closed the door she thought for a minute before she spoke.

"Maybe we should have told the cops we were coming down here."

Some of the girls nodded. The prospect of walking further down the trail into the darkness frightened them and offered little hope of producing any   results.   Marsha spoke.

"We should come back at sunrise. Then we will be able to see more."

Joanne reluctantly agreed.

"God Damn Bastard!" she said as she followed the girls back down the snow covered trail. "Who would do this to my daughter."

As they drove back to campus Nicki paged through Emily's missed messages and calls.

"She called her advisor at 11:47 a.m., and then there are a whole lot of calls, texts, and voicemail that are unanswered."

"Ok, so that will be helpful for the detectives, Nicki. Don't delete any of that."

Nicki looked over to Joanne who was gripping the wheel very tightly.

"Yes. Absolutely."

Back on campus suite nobody felt much like sleeping. At 11 p.m. the lead story on the local news was Emily's disappearance. The news station had used the photo that the campus policeman had taken. Eventually Nicki went into her bedroom and her friends slowly went back to their suites. Joanne tried to sleep in Emily's room but rest barely came and when it did it was only for minutes.

Chapter 10

At the Saturday morning briefing of the Erie County Sheriff's department the supervising officer went over the unsolved crimes and made assignments. When it came to the disappearance of Emily Verada, a case that he characterized as a missing person case, he reviewed the known and sketchy details from the campus report on the dry erase board. There were about six officers in the assignment room at the time and he gave the Verada case to Officer Marta Fuentes.

Fuentes, an Iraq war veteran, a talented boxer and mixed martial artist had been the first female hispanic officer hired by the department. She had been hired under a program of funding for local police by the Obama administration. She was tough, well-liked, and a hard worker. Her eyes were a kind brown and her skin was clear. She had a beautiful bright smile and was a devout Catholic. If you were her friend she would go to the end of the earth for you. She had earned the respect of everyone in the department.

"Sir, may I have the Verada case file?" Fuentes asked.

"We only have what the Mary Herman Campus Police sent over. There are some contact numbers in the report to get started. Officer Richardson will partner with you on this if it turns out to be anything."

Richardson nodded toward the supervisor and Fuentes. The officers knew that many of the missing person reports turn out to be false alarms or runaways. But those words were unspoken. They all knew that occasionally serious crimes were involved.   Fuentes smiled toward Richardson and acknowledged her supervisor. She sat politely through the meeting and planned her day.

At first light a group of hockey players, football players, Nicki, and some of the girls from the prior night gathered at Landing One in Price Island State Park. They walked slowly up the multipurpose trail looking for anything they could find. The snow on the trail had been plowed but the overnight wind blew some of it back. It was morning after a snowfall with the sun out warmly. The light that was created off the reflected snow was serene. The group made slow progress. They looked carefully on the trail and around in the wooded areas and down along the sandy ice covered banks of the Bay of Erie. One of the girls drove along on the parallel access road and offered the walkers a break from the cold every now and then. Later, when the sun was fully up, she drove over to the McDonald's on 26th Street and got some coffee and hotcakes for everyone.

Fuentes drove her squad car to the Mary Herman College to check in with the campus police. She needed directions to the small basement office of campus security. She entered through the glass door and introduced herself.

"Marta Fuentes, Erie County Sheriff's Department. I have the Emily Verada case."

The individual at the front desk smiled and led Fuentes back to the officers area. A uniformed campus police officer was talking on the phone but seeing Fuentes waved her in. She sat in front of his desk. He was entering information into a log book. When he finished he stood.

"Martinson. Jeff Martinson."

Fuentes stood and introduced herself. Martinson spoke with urgency. "I just got off the phone with one of the students. They have been conducting a search at Price Island and they have found a bloody headband." Martinson sipped from his coffee.

"I think you may want to head over there."

Fuentes agreed. She promised to come back when appropriate to be briefed by the campus force. She thanked the officer and headed out. On route Fuentes had dispatch patch her through to the Park Rangers to get coordinates. Eight minutes later she was at Price Island State Park and she pulled into the lot as directed. She moved forward and through the crowd to the young man who found the green fleece headband covered in blood about fifteen feet south of the multipurpose trail.

The Park Rangers briefed Fuentes as the State Police set up the crime scene. It was decided that they would use the State crime lab for forensics. Fuentes opened her small notepad and marked that that the headband was found fifteen feet south of mile marker 2.5 on the multipurpose trail in a wooded area that led away from the trail and toward a cinderblock building near the shoreline.

"Its a restroom and a changing station." One of the rangers explained as Fuentes walked the perimeter. The park ranger continued. "And it is unlocked during the winter months."

Fuentes nodded. She hypothesized that the attacker parked down beyond the cinder building out of site of passing road traffic, then made his way through the woods to attack Emily and drag her back to his vehicle. The troopers had taped off the area around the cinder building apparently thinking the same thing. On the southeast side of the building the ground was soft and the snow cover was light. Fuentes went to one knee and brushed away some of the drifted snow. She took in a deep breath and looked carefully. A bad septic system or maybe just luck but Fuentes was sure she spotted a partial footprint and some tire treads in the soft ground. She called out to the other officers who viewed her findings with satisfaction.

Within a brief period of time the various mobile crime labs had arrived and were gathering evidence. Fuentes prompted them to especially expedite the footprint and the tire treads. She returned to her cruiser and began entering information into her laptop so it could go out to the other agencies involved. While she worked one of the Mary Herman hockey players came over to her passenger door and she lowered the window. He was out of breath and spoke in gasps. "I found this Ipod Shuffle about twenty feet from where we found the headband."

"Good work. Let's take a look." Marta Fuentes led him to the trunk of her vehicle. She also had an Ipod that she used when she worked out in the gym after her shifts. Next to the first aid kit and the shotgun was a small backpack where she kept her personal belongings. She took out her Macbook Pro and fired it up. She found the cable connector for her own Ipod and connected it to the found device. The officer and the hockey player both read the small icon on the screen the same time.

"Emily's Ipod."

They looked at each other but said nothing.

Chapter 11

As light entered the room where Emily was chained she thought more clearly about her situation. She knew that she was not having a dream. She knew that she was not under anesthesia. She understood that she had been beaten unconscious by a monster, kidnapped, then raped. She understood that she was being held captive. Her thoughts turned to survival. She knew that her decisions now would help her get through her ordeal. She knew that many people would be looking for her. She just needed to survive hour by hour until she was found. Her denial was morphing into anger and it propelled her.

The room where she was chained was lit by a beam of sun which was coming in from down the hall. It was diffuse light, not bright, so she reasoned that it might be a plastic window or a dirty glass one. Possibly there was a stairwell, she thought. Emily looked around her room for anything that might help her. The floor was linoleum tiles red-brown alternating with grey. Some were peeling up. There was a dark corner that received very little light and it was populated by thick cobwebs and large, brown spiders. Above the door that opened to the room was a small vent that had been knocked out. It was about two feet across and about eight inches high. There was no way that she could fit through that space even if she could get free of the chain on her leg. A similar vent joined her room with the secretary's room next door, its louvered fins still in place. Left of the vent the floor was discolored and two capped copper pipes extended from the wall.

"It must have been a janitor's closet at one time." Emily whispered to herself out loud.

Below the pipes was a small box of papers that were stacked and had yellowed with time. Emily found that even chained to the floor she could move about the room if she stretched her leg. When she stood she felt dizzy so on her hands and knees she made her way to the box of papers. She flipped through technical charts that she didn't understand. There were invoices of various types. She concluded that the building once was a manufacturing facility. Under the papers in the bottom of the old box she found a large metal screw, a clear plastic bottle top, a small piece of duct tape, and a can of WD-40. The can was rusty. As she explored further she found an old pair of channel lock pliers. They were stiff but appeared operational.

In the next corner of the room Emily saw and old broom with badly tattered bristles. Despite her desperate situation she couldn't resist the urge to clean so with the broom and a few of the papers from the box she moved the urine, stool, and blood from the spot from where she had been sleeping over to the corner with the spiders. When she lay back down to take inventory of what she had found oddly she felt slightly better.

The light in the room became brighter and then faded, possibly the result of cloud cover outside she thought. She drifted off into a near sleep only to be awakened the sound of a mechanical elevator. She heard it land with a thump. She heard the doors open with a click clack and then heard the man come down the hall. She became completely still and felt her heart pounding into her neck. She became aware the light from the secretary's room.   It cast a corrugated shadow through the vent and across her floor.   The man rolled his contraption out and down the hall and inserted his keys in another door. Emily was nearly overcome as the odor from the room moved in her direction.

"Wake up Bitch!" yelled the man.   Emily was totally quiet. He yelled again. No response. Then Emily heard the man slam the door and move in her direction. But it wasn't her door he was opening. He was across the hall. She heard the screams and the crying. She heard the jangle and click of the shackles and then she heard the wagon being wheeled into the secretary's room.   She could see through the louvered vent the legs of the man. She saw his pants fall down around his boots and heard his grunting and thumping. The woman he had in the room screamed at first but they were screams that were increasingly soft and weak.

Chapter 12

Marta Fuentes sat at the table with her grandparents. She had lived with them in Erie since she was twelve years old. Something had happened at her childhood home in Texas. She refused to talk about it to anyone. She simply left to visit her grandparents and never returned. Her grandfather led prayers of gratitude and the three began a meal of arroz con pollo that her grandmother had prepared along with biscuits and juice.

"Have you heard anything, dear?" Doci asked. Fuentes called her grandmother Doci since she was a baby. Her real name was Doris but the baby name stuck.

"No, Doci." Marta answered. "My supervisor told me they should be releasing the budget proposal any day."

Doci passed her the biscuits and the butter. She refilled her juice. "I will be praying for you dear. I think it would be terrible if they lay off any officers."

"Well it all depends on the funding." Marta reassured.

"God bless you all." Doci responded as she crossed herself. "I don't want to see any layoffs."

Pa had been quiet. He looked up at Doci and she knew to bring him more chicken. They had been together 59 years. He spoke softly to Marta.

"What are you working on, dear?"

"The Verada case."

He took in a deep breath. He had read all the details about it in the Erie Times Gazette and watched the coverage on Channel 44. He was a diabetic and had been disabled for many years from a gaggle of medical issues. But his mind was sharp. And Doci took good care of him. He waited for Marta to speak, if she wanted to. She took a picture of the girl out of her chest pocket and handed it to Doci. Doci got Pa's glasses and handed them to him and he looked at Emily carefully. Marta finished her juice.

"There are about seven different agencies investigating this case. And I think on Monday the FBI will be getting involved."

Her grandparents looked at her proudly. Marta continued.

"The thrust of the investigation is moving toward the step-dad. Apparently he travelled to Erie on the day she went missing and has changed his story a few times."

"I know you've been putting in a lot of hours, dear." Doci observed. She filled Doci's juice glass and served more rice and chicken.

"I don't think it was the father." Marta continued. "His story is shaky but I don't think he would have kidnapped her."

Pa listened carefully. He said very little. He loved his Marta more than anything in the world.

"I'm working on a timeline, and I am interviewing anyone who was in the vicinity on that day, including the rangers."

"The rangers." Doci asked.

"Yes, Doci. Emily's running route goes by the Ranger Station at mile marker 2.3. There is a large glass window that looks over the trail. They were apparently having a meeting at lunchtime and may have seen her pass."

Pa nodded. Marta continued. "I want to talk to all of them to hear what they have to say. The Park Supervisor is arranging for me to do the interviews."

Doci brought out some apple pie with vanilla ice cream. She poured hot coffee for Pa and Marta. She cut and served the pie in the sizes she knew they wanted. The room was warm and the aroma just right. Everyone was quiet as they ate. Doci looked up at the bleeding heart of Jesus that was framed on the wall above Pa's place at the table. And she broke the silence.

"I pray to God we don't have any layoffs."

It was silent again until Marta spoke. "I'm going get this guy. People should be able to run in the parks in Erie without being attacked. I'm going fix it so he can't hurt anyone else."

Pa sipped his coffee and nodded.

Chapter 13

Emily heard the elevator and knew he was returning. She maintained a fetal position with her hands above her head like she saw them do on Animal Planet when the bear was about to attack.   She heard him moving around in the secretary's room and then wheeling the dolly down the hall. He moved past her door and past the room of the girl across the hall and opened the far door. And immediately Emily was hit with the smell. It wasn't urine, feces, or body odor. It was putrid and she was overcome by it. She tried to take deep, slow breaths but it was getting stronger. She heard the dolly rolling again into the secretary's room.

Emily had never seen a dead person before but she was certain that the girl in the far room had died. She wondered how long she had been in that room at the end of the hall without food or water. She wondered how many times he had raped her. She wondered if she had a family and who they were. She said a prayer that she would be taken straight to heaven.

She could see the man's feet through the louvers. She could see that he had put plastic storage containers on the floor by his feet. Then she heard the loud buzzing of an electric saw. She saw blood splattering on the floor and then heard the saw struggling as it moved through denser material. Emily had to look away. She couldn't bear to even watch this man's feet anymore. When the sawing stopped and it was quiet she heard the girl across the hall crying loudly.

Emily heard the man push the loaded dolly into the elevator. She could hear the doors close and the elevator climb to the next level. The crying had stopped and it was quiet in the area. A cold wind blew through the hallway and the odor seemed less. The light from outside had dimmed and Emily noticed blood spatter on the ventilation louvers that joined the secretary's room.

The man wheeled the dolly to the loading dock and moved the containers into his grey van. He locked the garage door from the inside and the metal entryway with a dead bolt. He hadn't driven far out of town when he noticed flashing red and orange lights brightly behind him. He immediately pulled over and looked forward. A uniformed Lillyville City Police Officer walked to his driver's door with his hand on his gun and spoke curtly. "License and Registration, please."

The man reached into the glove box to grab the registration. Despite the cold temperature he was visibly sweating. "What is the problem, Officer?" He handed him the registration, proof of insurance, and his Pennsylvania driver's license.

"Murtins, Mr. Fred Murtins. Is that you sir?"

"Yes, officer."

"Please remain in the vehicle." The officer walked back to his squad car for what seemed to be a long time. The lights continued to circulate on the roof of the car. Murtins tried to calm himself.   Finally the officer walked back to the driver's window.

"Mr. Murtins, is this your vehicle?"

"Yes, Sir." was the answer. He explained that he used it for his business.

"The reason that I have pulled you over is that your rear brake light is not working. I have written you a citation."

"Yes sir." Murtins replied. "I will fix that immediately."

The officer noticed the red splatter on Murtin's forearm. He looked closely and queried. "Is that blood on your arm?"

"No sir. It's paint. Red paint."

The officer rubbed his index finger across Murtin's forearm and brought a dab of the red liquid to his nose.

"It sure doesn't smell like paint."

"Well, its that new low VOC water-based paint. It has very little odor."

The officer was not convinced.   He saw the business sign on the driver's door of the van. He read it allowed.

"Arnold's Boat Yard. Indoor Storage, Boat Painting, and Repairs."

Murtin's replied. "Yes sir."

The officer handed him the ticket.   "Do you have any weapons or drugs in the vehicle?"

"No Sir?"

The officer persisted. "Do you mind if I look inside?"

"No sir. That would be fine." Murtins responded. The officer walked to the passenger door and looked under the seat and in the glove box. Murtins tried to distract him.

"Sir, do you have a boat?"

The officer smiled. "Yes. I love to go fishing in the summer. When and if it ever arrives."

Murtins smiled. "Let me give you my card. If you need storage or any repairs I can give you a great deal, seriously."

The officer smiled again. His demeanor seemed lighter. He opened the back doors of the van. The six plastic storage containers holding the chopped up body of Elaine Mary Angbright sat forward on the carpeted floor. They were taped shut with clear tape. She had been butted off her mountain bike on a desolate road near Findley Lake, New York about a month prior. Murtins had stalked her for some time waiting for his opportunity. She fell unconscious and was severely injured. He brought her to his boat storage facility like the others, raped her repeatedly and starved her to death. During her captivity he burned a number on her back, her buttocks, and across her chest. He wrote the number on a postcard and mailed it to the Findley Lake Chamber of commerce. They brought it back to the post office who gave it to the police.

"What's in the boxes?" the officer asked.

A bead of sweat appeared on the driver's brow. He smiled nervously.

"Oh, that's some engine parts. A Mercruiser inboard I am trying to rebuild. It's totally apart."

The officer persisted. "Do you mind if I have a look?"

Again Murtins smiled nervously. "No problem. Only I spilled some oil on the carpet earlier today, so be careful if you crawl in there."

The officer looked at him and smiled. He thought for a minute and then stopped. "You mean you would give me a deal on indoor storage, winterizing, and a spring tune up."

The man paused, smiled, and handed him his card. "If you could refer some business my way I could make you a really good deal."

The officer was now in an entirely different frame of mind and queried sympathetically. "Has business been slow?"

Murtins put on his best sympathetic face and paused for a long, quiet, spell. "I could always use a few more customers. I would appreciate anything you could do."

The officer noted Murtins bad eye. It was actually quite grotesque. He wanted to ask but stopped. Then he shut the rear van door. He looked down at the card and up at Murtins. "Ok, then maybe I will stop by. Are you at this address most days?"

"Yes sir, most days."

The officer explained that he would have fifteen days to pay the ticket and he would have to include proof that he had fixed the brake light. He walked back to his squad car thinking about that ugly eye, put it in reverse, and then sped around the man. Murtins waited for some time before he got back in his van.

He arrived at his New York State land about forty-five minutes later. He navigated down the long dirt road, partly covered with snow until he cleared the small stand of trees and parked by the shed. He unlocked the padlock and carried the plastic containers and placed them inside with the others. On his next visit he planned to take out his Bobcat and bury the contents of all the containers in the usual place under the walnut trees.   For now he stacked them along the tin wall arranged by the numbers that he had written on them.

He locked the door on the way out and proceeded back to the paved road. As he turned to head south he passed a farmer in a pickup truck. The farmer waved in a neighborly way. Murtins returned the gesture and whispered out loud.

"Stupid Cop."

Then he laughed out loud, turned up the heat, and headed back to Erie.

Chapter 14

Emily heard the crying of the girl across the hall and moved in the direction of the noise.

"Hey. It's OK. We are going to be OK."

There was a long pause. Emily spoke again.

"What's your name?"

Again there was a pause. Finally the crying stopped and Emily heard the girl trying to stand and come to the vent above the door.

"Julie."

"I'm Emily."

"Emily?"

"That's a good name."

"How long have you been here?" Emily asked.

"I can't remember exactly. At least a week. I haven't had anything to eat or drink and my memory is poor. He told me I was too fat and I needed to lose weight. That's why he said he was starving me."

There was silence for some time. Emily heard Julie move back to the floor in her weakened state. The crying started again. Emily moved to the vent and spoke louder.

"Julie, we are going to get out of here. I have a plan."

There was no response. Emily didn't have a plan but

she tried to stay positive. She looked around her room and took the pliers that she had found earlier and hammered the small screw against the capped pipe in the wall. At first nothing. She tried again. Nothing. She lay on the floor for sometime before she tried again. The smallest drip water came from the hole made by the screw. She grabbed the plastic cap and filled it slowly. When it was full she looked at it like a gift from heaven. She was so thirsty. But first she needed to help Julie. She had been here longer. She needed the water first.

Emily took the tape from the box and taped the cap to the broom, and moved close to the vent above her door that led to the hallway.

"Julie, I have some water. Push the vent open above your door."

Emily heard Julie struggling with the old broken vent.

"Hit it harder. I will pass the water to you."

After some time Emily heard the vent pop open with a clang. Emily guided the broom with the taped cup through her vent over to Julie's room and she grabbed it. She could hear Julie drinking, slowly at first, and then with a gulp. After a moment she heard a sigh.

Emily reassured. "Pass it back. I will send some more."

Julie drank again. She felt stronger. Her voice was clearer and she spoke.

"Thanks, Emily. I really appreciate it."

Emily filled her cup and drank for the first time. When she finished she felt slightly stronger. The water was warm but it was perfect. She taped the small leak closed and put her tools back under the papers. As she drifted off to sleep she let her tongue wet her lips and she swallowed again. It was the best water she had tasted in her entire life. The crying had stopped. It was now quiet in the building.

Chapter 15

Officer Marta Fuentes sat across from Emily's father, Derek Verada. He had agreed to return to Erie and to be fully cooperative. He was 47 year old. He had dark hair, grey at the temples. He wore horn rimmed glasses. There was something about him that Fuentes didn't like but she couldn't put her finger on it. She was the third investigator to question Mr. Verada. He was a successful banker and after his divorce from Emily's mother he relocated from Pittsburgh to Philadelphia.

Fuentes was professional but firm. She had read the reports of the other investigators. She didn't need to repeat all of the questions. She focused in a few areas.

"Mr. Verada, you had initially told the officers that you transferred planes in Erie and continued on to Detroit, but you didn't, did you?"

Verada looked away from her eyes. "That's correct. I wasn't in Detroit."

"Then where were you on Friday when Emily went missing?"

"I was in Erie."

Fuentes remained silent with her eyes on Verada. He took a deep breath and continued.

"As I told the other officer I have a friend in Erie, a banker, that I met last year when I was visiting Emily more frequently. Since she is a married woman I was trying not to get her involved in this whole thing."

Fuentes was silent. She stared at Verada.

He continued. "I have been coming here occasionally on weekends to visit my friend, but I haven't been in touch with Emily. I guess I feel guilty about that."

"Do you have a good relationship with your daughter?"

"Yes, of course. My problem has never been with Emily."

Fuentes paused and looked away. Then she wrote something in her notepad and continued.

"Who is your problem with?"

"My problem has always been with Joanne, Emily's mom."

Fuentes nodded to Derek Verada to continue.

"You see Emily had an older sister, Becky, who I adored. Before Emily was born Becky and I went on a canoeing trip in Michigan and we got into some rough water and the canoe capsized."

Fuentes nodded for him to continue. He was now revealing information that wasn't in the other reports. He took in a sigh, moved about in his chair, and continued.

"The water was cold. I panicked and swam directly to shore. Becky never made it. Her body was found a mile downstream. She had drowned."

Fuentes could see that a tear was welling in Verada's eye. She motioned for him to continue.

"There was an investigation. Of course I was never charged, but Joanne never forgave me. She told me I was a coward."

Fuentes queried. "Why are you telling me this?"

Verada paused for a minute. "Well after Becky died Joanne and I were never together again. I mean...."

Fuentes interrupted. "I understand, Mr. Verada. So you are not Emily's biological father?"

"No. But we never told her anything. We just stayed together as if everything was fine. I always loved her as my daughter. I would never do anything to harm her."

Fuentes believed him but gave no indication of her thinking.

"But you eventually got divorced."

"Yes. Joanne insisted. I know it was hard on Emily."

Fuentes gave Derek Verada a cold, long, penetrating stare and framed her question. "Are you involved in any way in Emily's disappearance?"

Derek Verada did not look away. He answered without hesitation and although Fuentes said nothing she believed him. She stood up and thanked him for his cooperation, told him he could leave, and suggested she provide him with the telephone number of the woman that he was with on the day Emily disappeared. Verada took out a business card and on the back wrote down the woman's number and handed it to her.

Chapter 16

Emily heard footsteps then the heavy motor of the elevator. She heard the door open and then she saw his feet in the secretary's room. He wheeled his contraption out and stopped outside her door. She heard the key enter the lock and the dead bolt turn. He held a club in his hand and he was ready to use it. She cowered as he lifted it above his head. He moved her naked body onto his wagon and shackled her arms and legs as he had done before.

Emily suggested. "If you let me free I could cook you some dinner."

He laughed. She continued. "If you would let me take a shower I would be more attractive for you."

He paused for a second and laughed again.

He wheeled her into the secretary's room and sat at his table working on something. Emily lay exposed, bruised, and weakened, strapped to his table. She didn't know what would come next. She only knew what had come before. He moved closer and then Emily felt a searing pain in the middle of her back. She let out a scream. It continued to burn. He was writing on her skin with a red hot wood burner. He was writing a number. She made out the number "two". And then the number "three". She was being branded like an animal. She was number "Twenty-three" She felt it first on her back and then on her buttocks.

In the room across from Emily's Julie heard the screaming and smelled Emily's flesh burning. It gave Julie the dry heaves. The pain was so intense that for a brief time Emily lost consciousness. The he went back to his desk. He was working on something. He turned to Emily forcing her mouth open and put a metal device in her that kept her jaw from closing. She could not bite down. Then he came to her and there was nothing she could do.

After some time he wheeled her back to her room, shackled her to the floor, and hit her severely on her leg with his club. Emily drifted in and out of consciousness. She didn't hear him rolling his wagon away. She didn't hear the elevator climbing to the next floor. She didn't hear Julie crying across the hall. She only knew she would be better off if she had died at Price Island Park.

Chapter 17

Fuentes tacked a construction board drawing on the wall of her bedroom at home. On one wall she had laid out a timeline. She started at the point Emily entered psychology class on the Friday right before she disappeared and continued up to the present. She marked the line with arrows connecting to known or reported events, such as her yellow VW found in Landing One by Ranger Matsos, or the finding of her bloody headband at mile marker 2.5. From these events she drew lines with people to interview, evidence to follow up on and the like. On the other board she had drawn a detailed map of the park with the multipurpose trail and the road and the wooded areas. She drew in the buildings and the parking areas. From various vantage points in the park she drew lines to her thoughts and "to-do" items. As she completed these items she made a thin red or green line through them, coded them with a letter and wrote her notes in a notebook by each letter. It was late and the house was quiet. Fuentes worked in cut-off army fatigues and a tee shirt.

Doci, realizing that her grandchild was still at work, got out of bed and put on some tea. She fixed it just the way Marta liked it, brought it into her bedroom and put it on the dresser.   She sat in her bathrobe and looked over Marta's work.

"I could bring you a muffin, dear."

"Thanks, Doci. I am fine."

Marta sipped the tea. It comforted her.

"You are staying up very late, dear. And you have to work tomorrow, early."

"I know. But I want to get my thoughts organized. The FBI people are coming tomorrow and a lot of agencies will be there."

"OK. Please sip some tea before it gets cold."

Doci handed her the teacup and Marta sipped. She took in a deep breath and went over some of the things she was working on.

"We should have some preliminary reports from the crime lab tomorrow, the shoe print, and the tire track. I will need to call first thing tomorrow."

Doci listened.

"And I will need to visit the elderly couple who thought they saw a silver van exciting at mile marker 2.6 at about the right time."

Doci counseled. "You will need to get some sleep."

"And I have three more park rangers to interview. The supervisor gave me a list of eighteen, but three didn't show. These are the one's I need to talk to."

"Maybe they didn't show for a reason."

"That's right, grandma. Maybe they didn't show for a reason."

Doci heard Pa turning in the bed and stood up. Otherwise it was quiet and warm in the house. She stood by the door with her hand on the knob.

"I will have some coffee, bacon, eggs and toast out for you at 5:45 a.m. Try to get some rest."

"Thanks, Doci. I love you."

Doci looked her right in her eyes. Her grandmother had gotten older over the years but her eyes were the same. They had never aged.

"I love you too, Marta."

Doci walked back to her room and settled Pa. The light in Marta's room stayed on for some time before the house finally became dark. It wasn't until Doci heard Marta snoring that she finally drifted off herself.

Chapter 18

Emily passed Julie some water through the vent. It was completely dark in the building so the girls had to work by feel. Julie was weak and it was difficult for her to stand. She had not had any food for over a week. Emily had noticed her daily deterioration. She sensed it in her voice and her cry. She was much quieter when he was away and when he rolled Julie into the secretary's room there was almost no noise. There wasn't a scream or a moan or the crying that usually followed. Emily knew that Julie did not have much time left. She knew that she could not last much longer without any nourishment given her daily torture. She knew that she needed to keep him away from her if Julie was to have any hope.

"What are you going to do when we get out of here?" she asked optimistically. Emily sensed Julie was smiling. She heard her gulp the water that she had passed.

"I think I will take a long warm bath."

"Yes, that will be nice."

"And sleep in my own bed."

"Yes."

"And hug my friends, and not go anywhere without them."

"OK."

"And maybe order a pizza and some diet Coke."

"What kind of pizza."

There was a long pause. Julie was weak. Emily waited. The rooms were dark and it was quiet. It was the kind of quiet that only comes in the winter when everything is far away. Emily waited some more. After a long while she heard Julie slide back down to the floor. She could hear the metal noise made by the shackle on her leg as it lay down with her. Then she heard Julie crying again. After what seemed like a long time Julie spoke in a soft dreamy tone.

"Double cheese with green peppers."

Emily considered her response and replied. "Yes, that would be excellent."

Julie didn't say anything else for the rest of the night. Emily whispered that she had more water and that it was important to drink but Julie did not reply. Emily held her breath and listened very carefully and she was certain that she heard Julie's breathing. She was determined to not lose Julie. She would do anything to keep her alive.

There was the slightest whiff of a cold breeze coming from somewhere and Emily was aware of it. Maybe there was a window that was open that he had forgotten to close. The breeze seemed to come into Emily's room and then became quiet. It was like she was being watched by the breeze. The sensation lingered for a while and then slowly left. Emily moved to her side, adjusted her leg shackle and waited. After some time she heard the train in the distance, more of a vibration at first, and then it became louder. She heard the click clack of the wheels and the bells of the crossing. After it passed she could hear it for a long time getting softer as it moved off from her consciousness. Eventually she drifted off to sleep.

Chapter 19

The room where the FBI regional task force convened was larger than Marta Fuentes imagined. She arrived early and watched from her seat as the other officers, investigators, and agency representatives shuffled in. She noted the high level of testosterone in the room, although the prancing and chest strutting by her colleagues was not new to her. When the FBI representatives entered the room the chatter softened. Fuentes planned to take careful notes.

The FBI team was represented by three individuals, two large males and an extremely well dressed female, who fiddled with her laptop before the meeting began precisely on time. Fuentes looked around the room and recognized individuals from the Erie and Millcreek Police, the Park Rangers, State Police, Border Patrol, Mary Herman Campus Police, and some units from jurisdictions she did not recognize. The tall FBI agent in the blue blazer cleared his throat and the meeting began. He did not use a microphone. He spoke with comfort and authority.

"This is the 7:00 a.m. scheduled meeting to coordinate the missing person investigation on Emily Verada, a 20 year old female student at Mary Herman College. My name is Agent Nickles.   With me are Agents Jeffreys and Sloan.

Agent Sloan is our criminal profiler and will give a presentation following my remarks."

Some of the officers seemed too big for their chairs. Others stood and sipped coffee. Fuentes took copious notes. Nickles continued.

"Within 75 miles of Erie city and in the last five years sixty-one females aged 18-24 years have been reported missing in your jurisdictions. Most of these cases have been solved, runaways, domestic disputes, psych issues, one known homicide. I know that you understand how these cases break down statistically. Unfortunately, over twenty of these cases remain unsolved."

One of the local detectives raised his hand and was recognized. "Erie is a medium sized city, and if you go out 75 miles, how does this compare to other areas?"

Nickles responded. "Number of reported runaways per capita- exactly as predicted. Number unsolved- highly unusual."

The detective followed up. "So what are you saying?"

Nickles responded. "We believe that you have a serial killer. We can't corroborate that with bodies of decedents or witnesses, but in that age cohort with that number of unsolved you definitely have a pattern."

The detective followed up again. "So why isn't this in the public's mind? I haven't seen anything in the papers?"

Nickles responded. "The victims have come from a wide area and over many years. Many have been college students and college administrators prefer to minimize this type of publicity. Additionally, we can't say definitively what has happened to these missing persons because we don't have any bodies yet."

Nickles put a map on an easel that showed the last known location of the missing women. The pins were color-coded by the year of their disappearance. Below joined by an arrow was a brief description of the circumstances, key evidence, and jurisdiction. Marta Fuentes and many of the other investigators wanted to be certain to get a copy of that map.

Nickles continued. "We believe the recent disappearance of Emily Verada as well as two other missing persons from Eastern Ohio and Southwestern New York State fit the pattern. That is why we will be coordinating and supporting this investigation."

He went on detailing how the various agencies would work together, report findings, share activity logs, forensic and criminal reports, and coordinate the investigation to avoid overlap. Fuentes felt good about this approach.

Nickles introduced Agent Sloan who she spoke from the podium in the front of the room. She wore a grey wool suite and shiny medium heels. She spoke in a confident and educated manner.

"We are looking for someone who likely is in his forties or fifties. He is highly intelligent and methodical. He may have a medical condition or a handicap of sorts. He is known to the psych community, and if he has a criminal record, it is probably distant. He was probably raised in a troubled circumstance, he may have been abused. He has managed to blend in among us, to stay under the radar screen. He is highly methodical and he is extremely dangerous."

One of the detectives raised his hand. "That could be a lot of people in the Erie area?"

Sloan continued. "Yes. Typically these individuals have a history of cruelty to animals, difficulty in school, antisocial tendencies."

Sloan continued in detail elaborating on her profile of this individual. Fuentes wrote as much as she could. She was very impressed by Sloan. When Sloan finished she took off her glasses and introduced the third Agent, Jeffreys. Jeffreys spoke in the front of the room with ease. He had a baritone voice and large forearms. If you were going to run right with the football you would want Jeffreys blocking for you, Fuentes concluded.

Jeffreys advanced the projector to include a number of postcards from places around the area. On the reverse was written in large and small print the same number over and over again.

"Here is apparently the signature of our suspect." Jeffreys pointed to the postcards on the projector. "He takes a young female from a location and then sends the a postcard to some local address only listing a number over and over."

Jeffreys walked to the front of the room and continued.

"We have fifteen of these cards at the present time. We don't believe we have recovered them all. It is likely some of them were discarded. We think the number relates to each of the young females he has captured. He appears to be bragging about this to the public. He seems to be saying "come get me if you can."

There was an audible gasp in the room. Officers and detectives don't like being taunted and for the first time many understood the gravity of these missing females. The meeting broke up with another scheduled for later in the week. There was coffee in the back of the room. Fuentes warmly introduced herself to Agent Sloan.

Chapter 20

A dusty beam of light came across the hallway and Emily stood looking outside the vent above her door. She concluded it was daytime. The building was dark, quiet, and cold. Julie had not spoken or moved for hours. There was no noise above and the elevator sat quiet, motionless. A wound was opening near the shackle point on Emily's left leg. A small amount of yellow pus formed along the open abrasion. She noticed a pressure sore opening on her left hip where she had been sleeping on the dirty floor. The wound on her back and her buttocks where he had burned the number "twenty-three" was less painful than the day before but was blistering and oozing a small amount of thick green fluid.

Emily knew these wounds untreated were dangerous. She considered herself a detail person. She would never let a wound such as the ones she had go untreated.

Emily thought of her grandmother and how much she loved her. She remembered when she was much younger the summer grandma and grandpa took her to Mackinac Island and they swam in the pool and rode in the horse drawn carriage. When grandma got sick and was put in a home it wasn't the stroke or the Alzheimer's disease that killed her. Rather a small sore on her hip from laying in bed and not keeping it clean. The wound got infected and the infection spread to her blood and a few days later Emily and her family had to drive to Michigan for a funeral. Even though Grandma was old there was a lot of crying that day. And afterwards Grandpa seemed lost. Emily remembered that he even came to Sewickley to live with them for a while, but without Grandma he didn't live much longer.

Emily felt weak from standing. She rested on her other side in the dark room, leaving her infected hip up to the cold air. She remembered when her father would come to her bedroom at night and tell her a story before she would go to sleep. She was in grade school then, but it was one of her favorite things. She told him that a story was necessary for sleep. When her father talked with his arm around her she felt like she would live forever. She remembered he liked to tell the story of the brave warrior who was defeated in battle, not because of weakness, but because of a problem with his saddle. The saddle was a good saddle but it didn't sit well on his horse. His horse was a good horse but he had a problem with his foot. It was a good foot but there was a problem with his shoe. It was a good shoe but there was a problem with the nail. It was a good nail but it had been put in at a slight angle. This bothered the horse and led to a limp. The limp caused the nail to come loose. The loose nail caused the horse to be unstable and so on. Emily knew that all the details mattered.

Right then Emily realized that she was going to die. Not because she had been kidnapped, or raped, or starved. Rather she had a small infection on her hip that was going to get into her blood. She felt a lack of air in her dark room. She felt extremely claustrophobic. She felt her heart race. She knew she had a fever. She needed someone to help her. She let out a scream and there was an echo. Then there was nothing.

Chapter 21

Marta Fuentes left the FBI meeting and immediately called the crime lab on her cell phone.

"I understand everything is preliminary. What do you have for me?"

She listened and responded. "Only blood from the victim. What about the footprint? What about the tire track?"

She listened. She took out her notepad and wrote furiously. "A Michelin Truck or Van replacement tire. Do you have the size or the model number?"

The crime lab person on the other end gave her the numbers. Fuentes wrote them down. She continued. "What about the footprint?"

Fuentes repeated his answer. "You said lugged sole likely size 10 1/2."

Fuentes listened carefully to the lab technicians verbal disclaimer. She grunted in agreement. She understood that it was not the final report. She understood that it could change. She knew there would be confirmatory tests. But she had something to go on. And the technician had more to tell her. She carefully took notes, then queried.

"Small fibers of ash wood in the girl's headband. What could that be from?"

Fuentes listened carefully then repeated.

"A club of some sort like a baseball bat or a broken oar. So he clubbed her in the head with something like that?"

The tech spoke.

"Yes, I understand. I appreciate it. I really do."

Fuentes suddenly had new energy. She felt her mind racing. She needed to make a plan for her day. There would not be much time. She opened her laptop and made a list of all of the tire stores in Erie Country. She mapped out a route for her visits. She remembered that she had three more people from the list of park rangers to interview. And on the recommendation of Agent Sloan she planned to visit the Warbler State Hospital to see if the psychiatrists would give her anything based on the profile.

On the central campus of Mary Herman College a special service was being held at the Catholic Chapel. Although the college was run by the Jesuits its namesake dated to the mid-nineteenth century and the order that Sister Mary Herman founded. Erie's oldest order dwindled over the years and in the 1970's the last nun retired from teaching. The college faced financial problems and that was when the Jesuits came to the rescue. Every square meter of the church was filled with students and faculty. It was late morning and it was dark inside. Candles flickered as the faithful bowed their heads in prayer. Fuentes moved quietly into the back of the church and crossed herself.

"What can we do to bring our dear friend back?" He asked. He was a white haired priest with glasses. He was very distinguished looking Fuentes noticed, probably a professor, or student advisor she concluded. He continued from the podium by the altar. He had a deep voice. It felt comforting.

"We can pray for the safe return of Emily Verada. Yes, prayer is extremely powerful. We can ask for God's intercession to light a path for Emily's safe return. We can pray here right now as an assembly and we can pray individually each and every hour until she returns. We can pray for the investigators who pursue this case and we can pray that if she is being held that her captor consider her release. And until she returns we ask you to grant her the strength that she needs for her sustenance. In the name of Jesus we ask for these things. Amen."

"Amen."

Warbler State Hospital was over an hour away and it was a long shot. But after visiting nine tire stores and fighting to get a busy clerk to research seven years of tire records she wanted a change of pace. She could return to her tire work later but she had scheduled an appointment with the administrator and one of the adult psychiatrists and she wanted to arrive on time. As she drove the grounds of Warbler State she concluded that it had the look of a Hollywood version of a mental hospital.

Fuentes sat in a ante room and waited for the administrator to hang up his phone. When he did he lit his cigarette and waved her in. Shortly thereafter a gaunt man who was disheveled appeared and lit his cigarette off the administrator's. He reached out his hand and introduced himself.

"I am Doctor Rashani."

Officer Fuentes explained to the two men her situation and the profile that Agent Sloan had built for her. She asked them for their help. Doctor Rashani studied Fuentes carefully. He eyed her from head to toe almost as if he had discovered a new species. Then the administrator spoke.

"We cannot release any patient information. Of course that would be a violation."

Fuentes queried. "Well, does anyone ever get discharged from here?"

The doctor spoke in a very soft voice. "Of course many patients are discharged. We have many success stories."

Fuentes continued. "Well could I show you a composite profile and a list of individuals and get your reaction?"

The administrator and the doctor met eyes and smiled as if they enjoyed the game. Then the administrator turned to Fuentes and nodded. Fuentes had compiled a list that included everyone that the FBI and the other agencies had interviewed, as well as many of Emily's friends and teachers at Mary Herman. It included the list of park rangers that the supervisor had compiled for her. And it included Emily's father. The list included about sixty names. She unfolded the paper and handed it to the administrator. Doctor Rashani walked behind his desk, extinguished his cigarette, and looked over the administrator's shoulder. There were announcements on the intercom in the distance. It must have been pill time, Fuentes concluded.

It wasn't long before both the administrator and Rashani were smiling like children. The administrator folded the paper carefully and handed it back to Fuentes. Then he spoke.

"I will need to call an aide to unlock the door to let you out."

"Yes. Thank you. What about the list?"

Dr. Rashani continue to study Fuentes in a way that she found offensive. She tried to ignore his behavior. After some time an escort with a bundle of keys arrived at the administrator's door.

"Carl, will you please take Officer Fuentes back to her car."

Fuentes stood. She wasn't sure if Carl was a patient or an employee.

The administrator and the doctor stood and Fuentes waited for either of them to say anything. Finally the administrator spoke.

"Of course we are not authorized to release any patient information unless we have credible and proximate knowledge of a danger to self or others."

"Yes sir, I understand."

"However, the doctor and I both agree that you have a very interesting list. And it might have even been more curious if you wrote the names on postcards and mailed them our way, if you know what I mean."

"Yes sir, I understand. Thank you."

"Of course he has not been a patient here for many years, right Doctor Rashani?"

Rashani smiled ever so slightly and nodded.

Chapter 22

The fevers were coming more frequently now and sapping what little strength Emily had. When they broke her body was quiet until the teeth-chattering, shaking chills began. She knew it was from the sore on her hip. But she couldn't move off of it. She lay naked on the cold floor, the open wound on her hip in urine and feces. She did not have the strength to crawl to the pipe and drink the rusty water. She only wished that whatever was in front of her would come fast and her suffering would end. She thought how wonderful it would be to have a blanket to wrap around her deteriorating body.

There was no noise from Julie's room and the dusty light that entered the hall had gone dark. Emily had wished she had fought with him days ago. Maybe she could have hit him with the pliers that she found or sprayed the WD 40 in his good eye. Now she was too weak to mount any kind of resistance. Now it was only a matter of time. When her fever spiked she drifted off into a delusional state unaware of who or where she was. In the brief time between fever and chills she had a moment to think, but when the chills were in full force she did everything in her power to not bite through her tongue.

She tried to remember how many days she had been in the room and how she initially got there. She tried to think of the things that were positive in her situation. She was young, and strong, and healthy. She had many people who loved her. They would be looking for her, she told herself. She had water from the pipe. She had found the broom, the big plastic cap and the small plastic cap. She had the pliers. She had Julie in the next room. She hadn't missed too much school yet. She could catch up, she told herself. And she could pray. She had forgotten to pray. Prayer was powerful she told herself. Why had she forgotten to pray?

Emily started to pray and she continued to pray as her fever rose again.   At some point her prayers became unintelligible and she drifted off into unconsciousness. When he came across the floor above and down the elevator she did not hear him. When he opened Julie's room and yelled at her calling her lazy she did not hear him. And when he took her into the secretary's room and had his way with her she was off in a distant place and was not aware of what was happening.

It wasn't until much later when she was awakened by the train, first in the distance, and then closer and she came to alertness.   He must have left a light on in the next room because now her own place was dimly lit in flickering shadows. The thing that she noticed, as if a huge weight had been lifted from her, was that the fevers were gone. She lay quietly in a pool of urine, feces, and dried blood. And in an amazing way she felt happy. The train moved off into the distance and then was gone. She crawled to the pipe, pealed back the tape and drank some warm water.

Chapter 23

Fuentes was up early. It was Tuesday, her day off. Doci heard her in the shower and quickly put on some coffee. When she came down through the kitchen she kissed her grandmother, took her coffee and the english muffins she made, and sat at the table. Doci sat with her quietly sipping from a small cup.

"I need to work out and then I am going over to Ohio to interview the parents of the girl who was reported missing three days before Emily Verada. Then I have three individuals who work at Price Island that I haven't spoken too as of yet."

Doci sipped. "Do you want me to pack you a lunch. I have some nice ham and cheese and some applesauce."

"Yes. Thanks. And a Diet Coke."

"Will you be home for dinner?"

"I'll try. I will have to see how the day goes."

"I'll check with Pa but I have a roast I could put in the oven."

"That sounds good."

Doci got up and walked down the hallway as Marta made her way to the door. It was dark outside and the white smoke from the neighbor's chimneys was visible. Before Marta closed the door she heard Doci whisper to her from the hallway.

"I love you, dear."

"I love you too, Doci."

Marta Fuentes lifted weights at the YMCA for about an hour and then took her mountain bike to Price Island and rode the trail at first light. She did not usually ride in the winter months, and with ice on parts of the trail she couldn't ride fast, but she thought it might give her some insight into the Verada case. And, as always, bike riding gave her energy.

At 10:00 a.m. she knocked on the door of the parents of Julie LeClair at their East Lake, Ohio residence. She introduced herself and they sat at the kitchen table. Fuentes took out her notepad and Julie's father began.

"Julie is our absolute joy. She has never been away for more than a week."

Fuentes glanced around the room. This was a working class family with a great deal of pride. The home was spotless and warm. The father, who had been off work at the local electrical supply store since his daughter had gone missing seemed distraught.

"Julie finished at East Lake High in June. She was class salutatorian." He struggled with the word. "She played varsity tennis and was all conference. She could have gone to a number of colleges, but money is tight."

Julie's mother put her arm on her husband's shoulder. He swallowed and continued. "So she started at East Lake Community and was working over at Wendy's trying to save up so she could transfer after a few semesters. She wanted to go to Princeton."

Fuentes probed. "When did she disappear?"

"Eight days ago today. Monday of last week." He looked to his wife who nodded. "Yes that's right. She would jog from campus down by the old boat yards and along the shore to keep in shape for tennis. I am told she went jogging a week ago Monday and we haven't seen her since."

Fuentes probed. "Did she know anyone who might want to hurt her?"

Bob LeClair replied. "As far as I know absolutely not. Of course the police questioned her boyfriend and her co-workers. So far nothing has turned up."

Fuentes probed. "Do you have a picture of your daughter?"

Julie's mother stood and brought back a picture of her daughter from her recent high school graduation.

Her father queried Officer Fuentes. "Do you have any new information to give me today?"

Fuentes paused before she answered. "No sir, I do not. Other than to tell you that the Erie County Sheriff's Department is investigating a similar disappearance of a young female like your daughter, Julie."

Bob LeClair looked down. A tear had welled in his eye. Fuentes continued. "And I am going to do whatever I can to bring her back to you."

At noon Fuentes knocked on the door of the private residence of Fred Murtins. He was scheduled to meet with her at the Ranger Station in Price Island but did not show on two occasions. This was the second time she knocked on his door. Earlier there had been no answer. Now she heard the dead bolt open and the knob turn. The woman who stood at the threshold was supported on a walker and Fuentes noticed that she was morbidly obese. Through the open door Fuentes noticed a school aged boy sitting at the table eating Cheetos.

"I am looking for Mr. Fred Murtins. I am with the Erie County Sheriff's Department."

The woman responded quickly. "He's not here."

Fuentes studied the woman. She was struggling to stand. She was breathing heavily. She was not old, Fuentes concluded, maybe in her thirties. The woman wanted to talk but had to catch her breath.

"Is he in some kind of trouble?"

"No ma'am. I just need to ask him some questions? May I come in."

The woman waved her in and Fuentes followed the corpulent female to the table where she sat with a sigh. Her son looked on with amusement until the mother berated him.

"Go on, get out of here. Can't you see we have company?"

The boy ignored her. He continued to eat Cheetos and fiddle with his Playstation.

Fuentes probed. "Isn't today a school day?"

His mother answered. "He's been sick. He has a bad stomach."

The boy left the room with a smirk. Fuentes sat at the table. The woman ate chocolate chip ice cream from the container.

Fuentes queried. "Can you tell me where your husband is?"

"Your guess is as good as mine. In the winter he works at his boatyard. Sometimes he goes out of town to pick up or return a boat. He usually checks in now and then."

Fuentes asked where his boatyard was. She told her and Fuentes wrote down the address. The officer handed the woman her card and suggested. "Would you give me a call if you see or hear from him? It is important that I talk with him as soon as possible."

Fuentes walked to the door and observed the woman. She tried to get up but fell back into the chair, short of breath. Fuentes acknowledged her attempt and started to let herself out.

Then she turned to the woman and queried. "Ma'am, would you happen to know your husband's shoe size?"

The woman smiled. "That's an easy one. 10 1/2 D."

Chapter 24

The next day Emily felt her strength slip away. She had called out for Julie but there was no reply. She tried to drink from the small pipe but she had no taste for the rusty water. The wound on her hip was draining a yellow pus and she thought she saw the bone exposed. The man had not been around. The building was quiet. Emily wanted to stand, take the broom and clean the pool of bodily fluids on the floor below her but she was too weak. So she prayed.

She prayed in gratitude for all of the good things that had happened in her life, for her mom and dad, and all of her friends. She prayed in gratitude for being an American and for being a woman and a college student. She prayed in gratitude for her good health and good looks and her success in college and sports. She prayed for Julie and she tried to pray for the monster who had taken her but she could not.   Mostly she prayed for a path out of her situation and if her prayers could not be heard she prayed that her suffering would be brief.

Her praying comforted her and redirected her thoughts away from her immediate predicament. The light remained on in the secretary's room and she could see around her cell. For the first time since she first arrived she noticed the spiders. There were many of them. More than she could count but she started counting them anyway. Some were going up, some were going down, and some were still. As she drifted off into sleep she expressed thanks that she had so many friends nearby.

Emily drifted from sleep to wakefulness for some time when she felt a licking sensation on her face. She instinctively rubbed her hand over her eyes but the sensation persisted. When she came back to awareness she was surprised to see a cat in her room purring as it licked her face. The cat had big eyes, one green and one blue. She had a full, thick, soft coat and a shabby collar without a tag.

Emily spoke out loud to her visitor.

"Who are you?"

The cat looked at her through slit-like eyes and purred.

"And how did you get in here?"

The cat meowed. Emily moved her legs and arms and verified that she was not dreaming. The cat must be a stray, she concluded. She must have found an open window in the building somewhere. Maybe she smelled the stench from her cell and came to investigate. She would have had to jump up through the vent above the door to enter her room, however. Yes, she could have done that. The cat didn't seem to be in any hurry to leave, Emily noticed. She took the plastic cap and crawled to the pipe and filled it with water for her friend and cat lapped it up. Her purring was quite loud.

Emily had an idea. She could take blood from the floor and write a message on a clear piece of the old yellowed paper in the box and tuck it under the cat's collar. Maybe someone would find it. Emily drank some water from the pipe and felt her strength begin to return. On a piece of paper that she found in the box she wrote in blood "Help! Emily" followed by the date as best she could remember. She folded the paper carefully and inserted it between the buckle and the loop of plastic that held the collar in place. Then with a renewed strength she lifted the cat, kissed her, and gently released her through the vent above the door. The cat, seemly knowing what to do, scurried away down the hall into the dark building.

At the Price Island Nature Center all winter mail was brought to the Environmental Building at the top of the hill. Someone there was supposed to look through it about once a week. In the pile was a post card that on one side had an aerial photograph of peninsula and on the other side had the number "23" written over and over in blue ink. The card had been postmarked in Erie the day before.

Chapter 25

Fuentes pulled up to the Arnold Boat Yard and Storage facility and parked her car. As she walked up the snow covered path to the steel door a brown, black, and white cat with a blue and a green eye scurried past her. She took little notice of it. She focused on the building. She knocked loudly on the door and no one answered. She waited and knocked again. Nothing. She was certain that she was on the right track. She needed to get inside. She walked around the building along a paved drive to a loading dock in the rear. There were tire tracks on the partially ice covered pavement. She tried to open the garage door but it was locked. She peered in the small dirty window at the side of the garage and saw many boats in blue plastic shrink wrap.

Fuentes walked the perimeter of the building and found no access. She dialed Fred Murtins's cell phone and the landline number on the door and got only voicemail. She left another message for him to call. Out behind the building was a dumpster. She took a walk over to it, lifted the lid, and peered inside. It was empty. Pick up must have been earlier in the day, she told herself. Before she left she searched the perimeter visually to see if there was a vantage point for her to observe activities at this building. She pulled her squad car to the neighboring abandoned warehouse and concluded that a camera on one of the second floor windows could monitor the steel door and the loading dock. She made a note of the building address and went back to her headquarters to prepare a petition for the placement of a surveillance camera.

As she entered the Erie County Sheriff's office dispatch gave her a message to see Sheriff Ackerman.

"What's this about?" she asked the young dispatcher.

"I don't know. He wouldn't tell me."

Sheriff Ackerman was the highest ranking official in the department. He had operational authority for the entire county.

"Is he in?" Fuentes asked.

"No. He is at a city counsel meeting."

Fuentes gave the dispatcher a concerned look. What could Ackerman want with her, she thought?

"He said he would be back at 4:30pm." the dispatcher told her.

"Thank you." Fuentes replied. "I will be back then."

The brown, black, and white cat moved from the Arnold Boat yard and up and over the wooden fence behind the dumpster over the railroad tracks and across the small industrial road that led to a large snow covered field. The snow was hard and she was able to move across it without sinking in. On the corner joining the main road was a gas station and a 7 Eleven and in the back was a line of dumpsters were she would stop to get a bite to eat. In the winter she got water by licking snow and she kept warm by entering industrial buildings. Across from the 7 Eleven was a road that led into a residential area and the cat followed it until she came to a schoolyard. School had let out and although many students boarded bright orange buses a few left on feet.

"I know that cat." said Sarah. "She's following us again."

Sarah, a 5th grader, walked home with her brother, Adam, who was in 3rd grade.

"Yeah. She's the one with the two eyes."

"You mean the two different eyes."

Adam laughed. Each of them had bright coats and backpacks. They sat on a rock at the lane that led to their house and petted the cat. She purred loudly.

"I wish we could have some animals." Sarah lamented.

"Yeah. Me too." replied Adam. "But you know mom is allergic."

"Yeah. I would like a cat, a dog, a fish, and a horse."

Adam agreed. He added a snake, a turtle, and an alpaca to the wish list. As Sarah stroked the cat she noticed the yellowed paper.

"Hey there is a message here!"

Adam came closer and read the blood stained message aloud.

"Help! Emily."

The two looked at each other and were uncertain how to proceed.

"Maybe we should tell mom."

"No. She would be mad if she knew we were petting a stray cat."

"Then what should we do?"

Sarah opened her backpack. She took out the wrapper from her sandwich and the Fig Newtons she didn't eat.

"Give me a cookie from your lunch box. I will put it with two Fig Newtons, a piece of clean paper, and half a crayon."

She carefully wrapped the package in the lunch paper, taped it closed and then to the cat's collar. Adam looked on curiously. He queried.

"Who is Emily?"

"How should I know?" was the reply. "But now at least she will have some food and she can send us another message."

Adam nodded in agreement. "Are you sure we shouldn't tell mom?"

Sarah looked him in the eye in the way only an older sister can. The two walked down the quiet lane and entered the back door of their two story house. The brown, black, and white cat followed for a bit and then tailed off to the north.

At 4:30 p.m. Fuentes waited outside of Ackerman's office. She had arranged for the surveillance camera to be placed on the second floor of the abandoned building near the Arnold Boat yard and had placed it there herself. She had even checked with the District Attorney's office to see if she needed any kind of approval to place the camera. They seemed to appreciate her thoroughness, she thought.

When Ackerman finally arrived she knew immediately by studying his body language that he didn't have good news. He signaled for her to enter his office and he quietly closed the door after her. She had a similar feeling the time in Iraq when their battalion was called in the office to learn of the deaths of six of their own. They had been out on patrol in a quiet section of town when they tripped an IED and it blow up their vehicle.

Later that night Fuentes sat at the kitchen table with Pa and Doci. She tried to explain to them there was nothing that could be done.

"It was funding promised by President Obama, in the stimulus, but it didn't come through. Four officers were let go. I wasn't singled out. We were all recently hired. The others had much more seniority."

Doci refilled Marta's coffee. She queried. "What about this case your working on?"

"He told me to give my activity log to Richardson."

"Richardson?"

"Yeah. He said Richardson would take over my active cases."

"But you have worked so hard."

Fuentes sipped her coffee. "They will give me a severance package, and he said he would write a letter."

The room was quiet for a long time. Then Pa shook his head. He queried. "A letter?"

"Yes, Pa. A letter."

Chapter 26

Emily nibbled on the Fig Newton and drank water from the rusty pipe and she was in heaven. It was the first food she had taken in days. She knew that she needed to go slowly and limit her intake. With two Fig Newtons and a cookie she felt that she could make many meals. Her cat stood by purring and lapped some water from the plastic cap that Emily put out. Before she ate she took the broom and pushed it through the vent and rapped on Julie's door but there was no reply. Emily recognized the smell that was beginning to fill the area and she was resigned to not being able to share food with Julie. It was too late. She named her cat Savior.

The nourishment brought Emily strength and with strength came anger. As her anger rose she focused on the man and how she could neutralize him. She would have no issue with killing him if there was a way. But most of all she needed to escape or be rescued. She focused on that. She thought about it for hours. She had the broom. She had the WD 40, or at least the empty container. She had a medium size plastic cap and a small one. She had the pliers. After her meal she wrapped the cookie and the remaining Fig Newtons in the old yellow paper and hid them deep in the box with the papers in the dark corner or her cell. She took the purple crayon and the blank paper and wrote a note.

"Emily Verada- captive and tortured. Middle aged man. One bad eye. Other girls killed. In warehouse somewhere. Hear train and crossing bells. Call Police. Send help!"

She tucked the message into Savior's collar, kissed her, and put her out the vent above the door. Savior looked back at her intelligently and then scampered into the darkness. Emily had stomach cramps from her first meal. She tried not to vomit. She knew she needed to lie still. She tried to lie perfectly still.

After some time she drifted off to sleep and in her dreams she was far away on a beach with white sand. The breeze was sweet smelling and mild. The water was crystal clear and slightly blue. She was on a team of some sort and the team had taken a break in this beautiful resort. One of the guys on the team who she liked had come down to the sand to sit by her on his towel. He brought with him some cool pineapple slices with toothpicks in them. Emily chewed on them and they were succulent, some of the pineapple juice dripped down her chin and onto her stomach. The sun was so bright it hurt her eyes. In the distance green mountains rose into the blue sky and small white clouds above. The two of them held hands, walked the path back to the pool, and jumped in. The water was clear and silky smooth.

Emily jolted to arousal from a far away place. It was the noise of the elevator. Then there was screaming. The elevator clanged to a stop, the door opened and the screaming was louder. He has another girl, she told herself.

There was a clean smell, like shampoo. In the hall there was a commotion and then she heard a door slam. Emily was fully alert now. She was focused. She heard him search for his keys and then she heard the dead bolt in Julie's door turn and the squeal of the hinges as the door opened. Emily smelled that characteristic odor that was pungent and now familiar and she heard him move Julie into the secretary's room. She was aware of the light being lit and when she heard the whine of the electric saw she turned away and covered her ears.

Chapter 27

Late February in Erie, Pennsylvania is often a grey time. The winter trudges on. The days are brief and the cloud cover low. Even for the people who have lived in Northwestern Pennsylvania their entire lives a longing for sunshine manifests at this time. The first blossoms of spring remain far from view and people bear the heaviness of it. Officer Marta Fuentes was acutely aware of her mood as winter wore on. She battled it with aerobic exercise, running on the treadmill, or playing pick-up basketball with her fellow officers. Years ago when she took a fews days in Orlando visiting her cousin she felt a lifting of the heaviness with a warm sun but she decided then that she wouldn't leave Pa and Doci. Now that her time was freed up she needed to revisit her plans for the future. With the dark sky above and a cold dampness in the air she preferred not to think about it. At the moment she preferred not to think about anything.

She turned in her gun, badge, and ballistic vest. She met with the human resources people and signed papers. She looked at the other officers who were let go for budgetary reasons. She knew it would be tougher for them, all men, some who had families. But she felt the pain of the separation and the sense of failure that came with it. She wondered if there was something that she could have done differently to preserve her tenure with the force. She told herself there was nothing that could be changed. She was, after all, a model officer who worked with pride and honor. But she doubted her own logic. It did not reassure her.

She made a deposit in her checking account, got a haircut, and visited her dental hygienist for a cleaning. It was as if nothing had changed in the superficial world of professional friendliness. How is everything, they asked? Everything is great, she answered. Could it have been that the truth was too complicated for her bank teller, beautician or hygienist? Maybe they too were close to a job loss in their family and if the truth was spoken it would infect them with bad luck. So, everything was fine, just fine.

She had lunch at home with Doci and Pa. Her grandparents were experts in reading Marta and would do anything to care for her. At the present, with the sudden shock of job loss, all they could do was to be present and that's what they did. Doci served homemade soup and prepared sandwiches with the ham that was left from dinner. The table was mostly quiet. There were many things that Doci wanted to say but did not say them. All she could do was stay on high alert for an opportunity to be helpful.

In the afternoon Fuentes met with Officer Richardson to go over her activity log. He had been hired exactly one year prior to the others and for that reason narrowly escaped the budget axe. Fuentes could have said a lot of things about his performance as a peace officer, but it was not her style to do so, and she realized that the department was by no means a meritocracy.

"So I have planted a surveillance camera overlooking the entries to Arnold's Boatyard." Marta explained.

Richardson smiled. "I heard that they are going to arrest the stepfather, probably today."

"How do you know that?"

"That's what Ackerman said his contact at State Police told him."

"What do they have to go on?" Fuentes queried. She was still in her role as an investigator.

"I don't know. I heard the ex wife ratted him out."

"Did they find the girl? What about the others?"

"No. Nothing like that." Richardson continued. "Ackerman is getting a lot of heat to do something. You know the college and everybody. If they could make it look like a father daughter thing then it might calm nerves on the campus."

Fuentes said nothing. Richardson continued scratching his chin.

"I personally think he's got nothing to do with it. But his arrest would seem like a break in the case. You know it would buy time."

Fuentes looked at him incredulously. Richardson continued.

"But I'll follow up on your boatyard surveillance. Don't worry about that."

He reached his hand out to Officer Fuentes. "Good luck with everything, and keep in touch."

"Thanks. I appreciate your efforts in the Verada case."

Richardson reassured her. "I'm all over it." He smiled and walked to the door, then turned to Marta Fuentes.

"Hey maybe we could go to dinner, or a movie sometime. Would you like that?"

Marta looked at him surprised. He was the last person that she would have thought would make a social invitation. She had no interest in Richardson romantically and she felt a little put off by his request but she didn't want to hurt his feelings. So she paused before she answered and then she spoke with feigned enthusiasm.

"Sure, Richardson. Let's do that."

Chapter 28

Emily ate the Cheetos that were wrapped in aluminum foil. She put the Pop Tart and the Fig Newtons in her hiding space. She washed the orange color off her hands and sipped some warm water from the rusty pipe. In addition to the food Emily read the letter that was neatly folded in Savior's collar.

"Dear Emily, My brother and I are thinking about you very much and want to come and rescue you. I cannot tell my mother about you because she would find out that I was near a stray cat and she would be very mad. My younger brother Adam (third grade) told his teacher about your letter and he got a lecture about making up stories so we are thinking about what to do next. Love and Kisses, Sarah and Adam. P.S. We will send in more food."

Emily turned to Savior and smiled.

"Do you want a piece of a Pop Tart?"

Savior purred contently and ate some crumbs from Emily's hand. At the moment that Emily felt Savior's rough tongue licking her hand she had a sense that she would get out of her predicament. She didn't know how or when but she had a positive feeling. That's when she heard the noise of the elevator. Emily heard screaming and whining as the man carried another girl into the hallway and chained her leg in the far room. She shielded Savior with her body. She tried to remain perfectly still. She heard the steel door slam shut. The crying was dull now and she heard the elevator climb away. Emily took out a piece of paper and started writing in crayon.

"Dear Sarah and Adam, Thank you for all your help. Here is the cellphone number of my best friend Nicki and my mom Joanne. Call them- they will help you. Love Emily."

She wrote the numbers on the paper. She carefully folded the paper and placed it in Savior's collar, kissed her, and placed her through the vent above her door.

Fred Murtins had not left the building. He was upstairs at his office desk and was reviewing his boat storage invoices. He needed to make an appearance at home to check on his wife and son and then he couldn't wait to get back to have some fun with his latest girl. As he worked at his desk he heard something in the rafters. He switched on the bright overhead light and spotted Savior walking along a supporting beam. He yelled up at the cat.

"Hey, how did you get in here?"

The cat looked at him and stood perfectly still. Murtins moved to the side of his desk and grabbed his .22 caliber rifle. He sighted it on Savior and pulled the trigger. There was a loud crack that echoed throughout the building and Savior moved out of sight, dripping blood from high above. Murtins shot again, this time hitting the cat just behind the ear, and after a brief soft whine she lay down on the rafter above. She did not move. Murtins smiled. She didn't fall to the floor as he hoped and he didn't have a ladder to retrieve her. He would get her down later he told himself. He shut off the light on his desk, locked the steel door from the outside and went home to check on his family.

In the far room on the floor Becky Parsons lay naked chained to the floor by her leg. She had been out jogging near the campus of Alabaster College in Muddy River some distance south of Erie. She was confused about what had happened because she had been knocked out with a wooden bat. As she came around she was certain that something bad had occurred. She screamed out for help. In between her screams Emily stood by the vent over her door and tried to console her.

Outside the dark clouds of the day had moved eastward and a few white lingering clouds covered the moon as if they were hanging from it. The wind moved with increased momentum across the darkness. The temperature had dropped markedly. Emily waited for the sound of the train and the crossing bells but it never came. She lay in darkness and drew a picture in her mind's eye of Sarah and her brother Adam and eventually drifted off to sleep.

Chapter 29

Marta Fuentes, now officially unemployed due to budget cuts, fished the lower Walnut Creek for steelhead. She waded along the grey slate riverbed until she found a good spot to cast. She put her fly rod across her body and let her bait of bright orange eggs sink in a pool across the current. In the winter months the steelhead migrate up the tributaries of Lake Erie and produce some of the best fishing in the region. There were other people fishing the river but Marta kept to herself. At the end of her day she had three large fish to take home for Doci to prepare.

Outside of Philadelphia in the small jail in the town of Ardmore Derek Verada sat awaiting transfer to Erie County. He was being held without bond until a grand jury convened on the charges of kidnapping and murder. Although the case against him was flimsy the fear in the community coupled with the frustration by law enforcement led them to want to do something. And it probably didn't hurt that in all the questioning by investigators Derek Verada came of as evasive and generally creepy, having travelled to Erie on the day that his daughter went missing to visit with his girlfriend, never having contacted his daughter. Law enforcement also was influenced by the fact that his first daughter had died under mysterious circumstances. But when Joanne Verada, his ex-wife, told police she suspected he was involved that was enough for them to move in and make the arrest.

Derek Verada was not without resources and he threatened a vigorous defense. His team of lawyers had already petitioned for his release. They cited the evidence gathered from a search of his condominium in Ardmore that produced some unsavory materials, however nothing that would link him to the disappearance of Emily or any of the other victims. For now it appeared to be a breakthrough for law enforcement and the local news outlets seemed almost celebratory.

There was one slight problem, however. As Derek Verada sat in a jail cell Becky Parsons went missing in Muddy River, south of Erie. She was young, attractive, and a runner. Blood was found at the scene of her disappearance and her abductions had all the markings of the prior kidnappings. There was no way that Derek Verada could have been involved with victim "24", if that was what she was. That bothered the people at the FBI.

For now the Bureau stayed out of the local law enforcement politics. They understood the need to arrest someone. It revealed effort. It was a sign of strength, not weakness. It calmed the community. And it bought time. But privately Agent Nickles, Jeffrey, and Sloan viewed Derek Verada as likely a distraction. They hoped that his arrest wouldn't slow efforts to find the actual suspect.

Fuentes climbed the steep bank to the parking lot at Walnut Creek. She changed out of her waders and noted the bright orange sunset. It felt good to run the heater on her cold feet. She turned the radio on and heard the reports about Mr. Verada. She turned the radio off. She wasn't thinking about anything now. She just wanted to go home and have dinner.

Doci made Marta's favorite fish dish but dinner was quiet nevertheless. Doci and Pa understood the stress that she was feeling and they did not mettle. To break the tension they talked quietly about nothing. Marta ate, remained until after desert was served, then politely asked to be excused. In her room she checked the timeline of the Verada case that she had crafted on her board. Next to it she had made a poster of her interviews and her to do list. Next to that she had a poster of the nineteen or so missing females that FBI Agent Sloan had given her. The girls in the small pictures were mostly smiling. They appeared young and carefree. Fuentes took down the timeline poster, the interview map, and the FBI missing female poster, folded them and put them in the trash by her night stand. She took her shoes off and even though it was early she lay across her bed and napped.

When Marta awoke she surveyed her wall and noticed its emptiness. The visual plan was gone but her emotional ties to the case were not. She opened the drawer to the night table and took out an envelope. Inside were two pictures, the first Julie LeClair, of East Lake, Ohio and the second Emily Verada of Sewickley, Pennsylvania. She looked at the pictures for some time and remembered the promises she had made to Mr. and Mrs. LeClair and to Joanne Verada. She dialed Richardson on her iphone.   "Not to meddle. I was interested in what the surveillance tapes showed."

He hadn't looked at them. He was happy to hear from her however, and it resonated in his voice. "They arrested the father, you know. I got busy with other things."

Fuentes was surprised. She queried. "Do you mind if I look at them?"

"Be my guest. If they turn up anything just send me an email. I can follow up. Let me give you my password, just in case yours was terminated."

Fuentes would need to log in to the Police Audio Visual Site to scan through the tapes. Richardson gave her his password. He continued with a chuckle.

"They also referred me to a third grader who says his cat knows where the victim is? I phoned his parents and they told me he has a wild imagination. I couldn't get out to talk to them today."

Fuentes consoled him. "If you wouldn't mind I could talk to him."

"That would be great. Hey, by the way, we all miss you down here."

Fuentes knew what was coming. She just wanted to focus on the case. Richardson queried. "You know you promised we would get together. How about Saturday evening?" Fuentes paused for a moment. "Let me see what these tapes and this young child interview turns up. I will be in touch."

"OK. But keep Saturday evening open?"

"OK. Take care."

Fuentes felt energized. She turned on her laptop and logged onto the Sheriff's Audio Visual Site.

Chapter 30

Emily dreamed of taking a hot bath. She imagined lighting scented candles and hearing the tub fill briskly. She dreamed of wandering about in a warm room in a white terry cloth bathrobe and looking at herself in a full length mirror. She imagined stepping into the deep hot water and wondering at first if it would be too warm but then feeling the muscular relief as she slipped fully in. She could almost taste the renewal as the hot water dripped over her abdomen and in between her toes. She sensed the silkiness of the shampoo and conditioner through her hair and how that felt. She dreamed of the sea salts that she had at her parent's house in Sewickley and how they soothed her aching muscles. She imagined the feeling of letting her head fall back into the warm soothing place where she all but disappeared, leaving only room to breath from her nose and mouth. She imagined a vanilla scent filling the room and all her cares a million miles away. And when the tub cooled ever so slightly she imagined turning the big hot knob with her toes and heating the water again.

There was no bathtub in her room in captivity. She had no terry cloth robe nor scented candles. There was no warm water to run across her abdomen and through her toes. She had a small piece of a Fig Newton and a small cup of warm, rusty, water. There was a draining wound on her left hip and a tight shackle around her leg. The bruises on her thighs and the bright red scarred number "23" on her back and across her buttocks were healing marginally. She lay in urine, feces, and blood. The blood came from her groin where he had injured her and from the back of her head. She had become used to the fevers now, or they had become less. All fear had left her hours ago when she knew inevitably she would die like the others. But she wasn't becoming weaker any more. She was becoming stronger, or so she thought, and more angry.

She had tried to console the girl in the distant room. Becky Parson, a college sophomore from Alabaster College in Muddy River, had been taken forty hours earlier. She was fully conscious now and terrified.   As far as Emily could tell he hadn't come to rape her yet. Emily tried to pass her some water but the room was too far to reach being at the end of the hall so she sang to her until she was quiet.

When Emily heard the footsteps above and the mechanical sounds of the elevator she knew what was coming. From the deepest recesses of her angry mind she sprung into an almost involuntary action. Emily was protective by nature and would stand up if she perceived injustice, but what motivated her at that moment she will never know.   She grabbed the small red plastic cap from under the papers and reached out and placed the largest brown recluse spider on her palm. Then she let it crawl into the red cap. She was mildly amused how well her friend fit in the cap as if it was her home.

Then as if she were inserting a tampon, she placed the cap inside herself and waited.

The man walked noisily past her door and toward the room of his next prize, but before he could open the dead bolt Emily spoke out.

"Hey Mister, I need you to give me sex. It has been almost two days. Come over here and get me please."

There was silence in the hall. She could hear the key slide out of Becky Parson's door and then into hers. She didn't see him smiling but sensed it. In an instant he slammed her onto his contraption, strapped her down, and wheeled her out of the room. As they left she briefly looked at the web of spiders in the dark corner of her room. In the secretary's room he had his way with her. She prayed that her plan might work and that he might be injured enough that Becky would be spared, at least for a few days. When he was finished she heard him whisper.

"Jesus Christ! Something bit me!"

She sensed that he was rubbing himself with a towel and then he wheeled her back to her room and shackled her to the floor. He didn't bother with Becky and left via the noisy elevator. It was quiet in the girl's rooms for hours. Emily couldn't be certain when the day ended and the night began but she waited until she heard the sound of a train, first almost imperceptibly, and then with certainty. She heard the crossing bells and it was loud and Emily sensed that despite her circumstances she was getting stronger every minute.

Chapter 31

Fred Murtins sat behind the curtain at Saint Veronica's Hospital in the Emergency Room. He had been waiting for what seemed like hours before a nurse led him back and asked him to strip from the waist down. Finally a physician pulled back the curtain and smiled.

"Mr. Murtins?"

The doctor was accompanied by a younger medical student. She was attractive and appeared tired. Murtins tried to read her name badge without being too obvious.

"Yes, that's me." he replied.

"The triage nurse says you have an infected penis?"

"Well I think something bit me."

The doctor looked puzzled. "Do you have any discharge?"

"No."

"Blood?"

"No."

"Burning with urination?"

"No."

"Trouble with intercourse?"

"Yes, because of the swelling"

For the first time Murtins looked up and the doctor noticed his opacified eye. He immediately queried.

"What happened to your eye?"

Murtins paused and then answered reluctantly. "I was poked with a hot piece of iron when I was a kid."

The doctor followed up. "Who did that?"

Murtins appeared a little upset. He hadn't come to have his eye evaluated. "Yeah, I don't remember." He couldn't bear to say it had been his own father.

The doctor asked him about his health history and medications and Murtins listed a number of psychiatric medications that he was supposed to be taking. The doctor put on a rubber glove with a snap and pulled back the gown to reveal Murtin's penis. The medical student shuddered and almost looked away. She said nothing. There was a small central blackened area where the spider had bit him surrounded by a red, inflamed, raw circle around it. It was quite swollen. It was draining pus. The doctor moved his organ in a number of directions and then began his line of questioning again.

"Any fever or chills?"

"No."

"Are you allergic to anything?"

"No."

"Well than I would like to check your white blood count and give you an intravenous dose of an antibiotic. It would probably be wise to have you seen by a specialist. Let me see what I can arrange."

Murtins started to stand. The doctor spoke. "No, wait here. We will get things started right away. That is a nasty bite you have there. Nasty."

Murtins nodded. The doctor and his medical student moved out and closed the curtain as if actors in a play. Murtins cursed under his breath. Back at the nurse's station the doctor turned to the medical student.

"That is a ripe wound he has. I may have urology look at him. If his white count is up he needs to be admitted. What did you think?"

"I agree. The guy was creepy. Did you see how he was looking at me?"

"You are right. But we specialize in creepy here. While we are waiting for his labs go down to medical records and pull out his hospital files and look them over. See if anything turns up."

Murtins had his blood drawn and got his initial dose of antibiotics from a clear plastic bag that hung from a pole at his bedside. The medical student walked down the dark hallway toward medical records, swiped her badge to enter, and looked up Murtins in the medical records computer database. She was amazed to see that he had been admitted seventeen times prior to the locked psychiatric unit. She moved deep into the record's room and retrieved four thick charts, piled them onto the cart and wheeled them into the small dictating room that physicians used during the daytime. There she could read without interruption.

A nurse circulated into Murtin's room to check on his intravenous. He queried pleasantly.

"I am real anxious to have a smoke. Can I go outside for a few minutes."

The nurse looked at him and at his I.V. "This antibiotic has another twenty minutes to run. Can you wait?"

"I don't think so. Smoking is a terrible habit."

"Tell me about it."

Murtins smiled. The nurse gave him permission and told him to take his jacket.

In the record room the medical student looked at the oldest dated record first. It was from nearly seventeen years prior.

"Murtins, Fred (Also Known As Ivanovich, Fyodor), age 17 years."

There were pages of demographic information followed by a large orange insert that read:
"Confidential Psychiatry Record- Not part of Medical Record. Do not Photocopy."

The medical student knew she had no right to review his psychiatric records. He didn't present with any psychiatric complaints. She wasn't on a psychiatry rotation. But she knew she wouldn't get caught. There was no one else nearby. She could say that she was only reviewing his general records for the Emergency Room as she was instructed to. She would return the charts to the exact rack where she found them. No one would know. She turned the page slowly and began to read the psychiatric summary.

A seventeen year old male- parents: father from Ukraine working for US Government. Father murdered and dismembered mother, then tried to blind patient with hot iron.

Father was eventually executed by State of PA. Patient in and out of foster care and juvenile criminal system. Charged in the disappearance and death of one of his foster step sisters but never convicted. Body of the young woman never recovered. Name changed to Fred Murtins as part of an Accelerated Criminal Disposition. Released and records purged. Plan to return child to extended family in Ukraine if social services and federal authorities can arrange.

Diagnoses: Sociopathic Personality Disorder, Schizo-Affective Disorder Psychiatric Course: Inappropriate for our facility. Plan: Transfer to Warbler State.

From outside Murtins could see the medical student in the light of the record's room. He watched her sitting and reading. He watched her running her fingers through her hair and twirling it nervously. He wondered how she would walk back to the Emergency Room. He felt his pulse quicken.

The medical student felt suddenly anxious, as if someone were watching her. She looked around. It was dark and it was quiet. She rolled the cart back down the records room hallway and placed Murtin's charts back exactly were she found them. Walking back to the Emergency Room she left the building by one of the fire doors and walked across the parking lot to breath fresh air.

When she walked by the van on the edge of the lot she didn't have time to scream or call for help. She briefly saw the man in the overcoat, she sensed the baseball bat flying toward her head, she sensed a softness about her skull, and she was asleep. Murtins duck taped her arms and legs, stuffed a rag in her mouth and taped it shut, pushed her into the van and covered her with an oily blanket.

Inside Murtins waited some time before the nurse returned. She checked his vital signs and when she took his pulse noticed blood on his arm and remarked.

"How could they start an IV and not clean up the blood?"

She wiped up the blood on his arm with a alcohol wipe, apologized for the IV teams sloppy care, and gave him his instructions.

"I have good news for you, sir."

Murtins grunted in anticipation.

"We spoke with the urologist and he said you will not need to be admitted. We will schedule you for daily IV therapy at our outpatient center and he will see you in his office. How does that sound?"

Murtins replied. "That will be fine. Thank you."

He followed her to the registration area where she went over his discharge instructions in detail. Then she asked if he had any questions. He thought for a moment and spoke with a smug smile.

"No. If I have any problems I have a doctor nearby."

The nurse looked at him puzzled. He folded the written instructions and left Saint Veronica's Emergency Room.

Chapter 32

In the days that followed Emily Verada's disappearance the campus of Mary Herman College was practically in lock down.   Extra police were quickly brought in and they maintained a presence throughout the campus. Many of the female students would not even walk to class without an escort.   Price Island Park, quiet in the winter months, had virtually shut down.   The area where Emily had run and was abducted was cordoned off as a crime scene.   Runners and walkers found other parks to visit or they stayed home where they felt safer. The local TV affiliates and the newspapers ran daily stories on the abductions.   Every young woman in Erie feared they would be next.

When Erik Verada was booked the story was reformulated as a domestic incident rather than a random act and the campus and town exhaled slightly.   But the students and the townspeople were suspicious of their news sources and remained on edge. After all no body had been recovered. And what about the other young girls who had disappeared? When the story of the missing medical student at Saint Veronica's broke the entire city went entirely into another fear dimension.

The rear parking lot of St. Veronica's was filled with reporters from the national media. A small village of satellite trucks seemed to bloom across the snowy field where they were instructed to park.

Erie, Pennsylvania in February can be a difficult destination. And when Tom Ridge Field was closed due to inclement weather the reporters came in rental cars from Pittsburgh and Cleveland. The local hotels, cafes, and bars enjoyed an increase in business for all the wrong reasons, but in Erie's economy any increase in February was welcome. Even the New York Times ran a story about the case, citing a Boston researcher that linked horrific crimes with a lack of sunshine. But despite the pomp, circumstance, reportage, and theories, no one was any closer to finding any of the victims.

Marta Fuentes downloaded the surveillance tapes from the Arnold Boat Facility that had been recorded over three days. She used Officer Richardson's ID and Password, and although he gave her the go ahead, she felt uncomfortable doing it. She knew she wouldn't get caught, and if she did he would definitely back her up. But she was no longer on the force, and technically it was a violation of policy. She knew he would ask her to dinner again and she would have to go. Even though she did not have a romantic interest in him she would play along if it helped get closer to solving the case.

She opened her Macbook Pro and clicked on the downloaded tape, resized the screen and watched. For a few minutes she saw a dark screen and flashes of light, then white out. She fast-forwarded through the tapes but nothing was there. Something had been wrong with the camera or the digital processing.   There was nothing to see.   No data had been recovered.   She decided that she would drive over to the surveillance site and examine the camera, but she told herself it could wait until the morning.

After about three hours in bed without a wink of stillness she sat on the edge of her mattress.   She slipped back into her jeans and sweatshirt and tied her boots.   She put on her black North Face down jacket and grabbed her Glock 9mm pistol and put it in her rib holster.   She had a good flashlight in her old Toyota Pickup.   As she turned the key it cranked slowly in the cold air.   She noticed that Doci had come to the window and pulled the curtain a sliver to investigate.   She was crossing herself. Marta blew her a kiss and sped into the night.

Chapter 33

Emily lay on the cold, stained linoleum floor tethered to a metal chain at her ankle. Her visitor, Savior the Cat, had not been by for days. Her fevers had returned. She had no interest in drinking the rusty water. Why hadn't someone come to get her, she thought. Where were the Police? Where was Nicki and her friends? Where were her mom and dad? Had everyone forgotten about her? Did they just leave her there to be beaten, raped, and then starved to death? Where the hell were they?

She knew that she could no longer think straight. She could no longer stand. She was too weak. She heard the other girls screaming and crying. She heard the girl from Muddy River and she heard the doctor. But she could not do anything. She was tired of fighting. She wanted to die. When she was dead the bastard couldn't hurt her anymore. Where the hell is everyone, she asked? Emily was not afraid to die. God had given her a good life she told herself. She could have died when she was a baby and she had meningitis and was in intensive care but God did not want to take her then. She could have died when she was a toddler and the house was on fire but somehow she got out. She could have died in sixth grade when she fell off the jungle gym and was knocked out.

Why didn't she die then? She could have died in high school at the cross country meet when the brakes failed on the bus and they went down in the ravine. Why didn't she die then?

Emily could feel urine running down her leg. It was warm and smelled foul. There was just a small amount. She was too weak to wipe herself clean much less move to the pipe and drink some water. Maybe when she was dead someone would clean her up she reasoned. Where the hell is everyone? She heard the doctor screaming for help. She remembered when she was strong and could scream like that. She remembered running along a trail and passing some slower girls and then moving fast up the hill and around the turn. The wind was blowing in her face but she was not slowing down. It was at that moment that she decided that she wanted to get married one day and have children. She knew she would be a good mother. Now she just wanted to die. Where the hell is everyone?

Emily lay nearly still. She was not aware of the cold floor, nor the lacerations on her leg from the chain. She was not aware of her fevers and chills. Her teeth chattered as her body fought the rigors but she didn't know it. She did not sense her nakedness nor the stench that enveloped her. Blood ran from her nose and her rectum. Her skin had become waxy and her eyes were sunken. Her hands and feet were puffy and blistered. A spider crawled across her chest and rested.

In the distance, softly at first, and then more powerfully, the rumble of a freight train became louder and louder until the bells at the crossing rang and the noise was at a crescendo. It must have been a cold, clear night because the sounds of the train were particularly pure.   The building shuddered and then the noise passed into the dark of the night and was gone. Emily Verada lay motionless and unaware.

Chapter 34

Marta Fuentes parked her Toyota Pickup behind the abandoned building in the lot adjacent to the Arnold Boat Yard. She made her way up the snow covered steps and entered through a rusted metal door that she was able to easily push free. There was a mattress in the corner, drug paraphernalia, and spent needles covering the floor. Nothing looked recent to her. By the door she noticed a heavy steel shovel and a crowbar. She figured they had been used originally to pry open the door. She tried to avoid stepping on the needles as she climbed the metal stairs.

At her vantage point on the third floor she looked down over the entrance to the boat yard. She could clearly see the steps leading to a steel door and the driveway that led to a loading dock. Both were quiet. The camera appeared to be in fine working order but the little red activity light was off. Fuentes fiddled with the batteries. Maybe they were bad, she reasoned. She saw no place to charge the batteries. She needed to take the camera home and charge them.

Fuentes sat on an old chair and peered out the window. There was nothing. She watched the door for a long time and waited. Nothing. She found herself nodding off to sleep but kept staring. She was sure she was on the trail of her suspect. Now was not the time to rest. She sensed that something would happen. Her tiredness was overwhelming but she tried to keep watching. Eventually the dull coldness and lack of activity began to weigh on her. She stood stiffly, looked some more, then left.

In the morning Doci came to wake Marta. She was embarrassed that she had slept so late. She put on a bathrobe and came into the main room. Pa had the television on and called Marta over. The news had spread like wildfire through the law enforcement community and then into the public. Even though the reports were not confirmed the local media wanted to be the first to cover it. The attractive reporter from WSOI stood outside the courthouse and spoke into the camera. The morning sun was bright in her eyes and the wind occasionally blew hair across her face.

"In a bizarre twist to an already challenging case the father of missing Emily Verada has apparently hung himself in his cell in Ardmore, Pennsylvania. Mr. Derek Verada had been arrested in connection with the disappearance of his daughter three days earlier and was awaiting transfer to Erie. We are unable to confirm any further details although there is a report that a long letter written to Emily was found with Mr. Verada."

Marta moved closer to the television and viewed the report. She shook her head. Doci put coffee and hot cereal out for her. She put some cinnamon buns in the oven. By now the local television reports had shifted to the weather. A cold front was coming across the lake and likely bringing moisture in the form of snow. Pa didn't need the weather report. He could feel the drop of the barometer in his bones. He had moved to the kitchen table were he was lining up his morning pills.

Chapter 35

The prosecutor handed Derek Verada's suicide note to the defense attorney.   In a gesture to the dead man's representative the prosecutor spoke.

"I am not certain that he was our guy."

The defense attorney nodded.

"Especially in light of the two similar abductions since his arrest."

"You've got a point there, my friend."

Arrangements were being made to move the decedent to the morgue. An internal investigation was promised. There were a number or legal and logistic issues to be addressed. The two agreed to work together.

The defense attorney sat in a coffee shop across from the courthouse and read Derek's last letter.   He sipped a vente latte with a small amount of cinnamon and added sugar. One of his feet slipped out of his shiny brown loafer and he felt the warmth of the fire on his back.

My Dearest Emily,

Of course I would never do anything to harm you. My daily prayers are for your safe and speedy return. The suggestion by your mother, or anyone else for that matter, that I might have had anything to do with your disappearance is completely false and I don't have the will to rot in prison while the public hangs me for a crime I did not commit.

I am not a perfect man. I have more flaws than most, and I alone am the source of most of my shortcomings. I have always loved you and will always love you and pray for your happiness and safety everyday. I write you now so you will know some truths that have burdened me for a long time. After some things your mother has said I know you wondered if I was your biological father. Now I will tell you I am not. But I have raised and supported you as my daughter and my love transcends biology.

The day your older sister died my life changed forever. The water was cold and the breeze was strong and when the canoe tipped I swam to shore like a coward. I am so sorry and I have relived the day a thousand times.

After your sister's death your mother never let me back into her life. Of course I was there and we looked like a family on the outside, but inside everything was cold and gone between us. She never forgave me for that day. You may already know that it was her boyfriend and not me that was your father. Maybe he should have raised you. But I loved you and wanted you to have everything your sister could not.

Now I have failed again. You are missing and no one knows why. My life has become a burden I can no longer bear. This will be the last letter I am able to send.

With much love always., Dad.

The attorney slipped the loafer back on his foot. He had hung his suite jacket nearby on a hook and he put it back on carefully. He checked his watch and his blackberry. He had time. He took a last sip of his expresso, now extra sweet with all the sugar at the bottom. He placed it on the tray with the other mugs. He took the letter, folded it in fours and then again. He tore it down the center and let all the pieces sink into the trash bin.

Outside it was cold and bright. The sun had melted some of the snow and the sidewalk was wet in spots. There were only a few fluffy clouds high in the pale sky. Icicles had formed on many of the buildings and there was the sound of dripping water. He slipped into his Mercedes, maneuvered out of a tight parking spot, and sped away.

Chapter 36

Joanne Verada met her attorney friend at the entrance to the Sewickley Club. The luncheon was a buffet and they took a sunlit table in the distant corner of the room. This was acceptable protocol in the winter months or if members wanted to meet and have a private conversation. In February lunch was served as a buffet with table service for drinks, coffee, and deserts. Joanne chose the cob salad with a small portion of wild rice, wrapped ham, and clam chowder. Liz had a pita wrap, chips, and a diet coke. In the summer the two had paired to win the women's best ball tournament. Each had done reasonably well in the second flight individual women's competition, and in the early days when Joanne was with Derek and Liz was with her first husband, they played in the evening couples' golf league. They had a lot of fun in those days, with golf, their husbands, and the young kids. Everything was quite different now for both of them but they remained friends.

"I don't know what they put in the potato salad." Joanne said. "But it has a sharp flavor."

"It could be the lemon pepper. They use a lot of lemon pepper." The attorney reassured.

Joanne nodded. Over Elizabeth's shoulder she could see along the 10th fairway with the beautiful elevated green covered in snow.

Liz continued. "Joanne, I'm so sorry for your loss."

"Yes." She looked up from her salad.

"And per your instructions I have had Derek's attorney fax me a copy of his will."

Joanne nodded and took a sip of her drink. She first met Liz at a neighborhood pool party many years earlier and she was immediately certain that they would be friends. It only seemed natural when legal matters arose she would rely on her in that capacity. After all Derek had been her family banker. She even wondered at one time if Liz had an eye for Derek. Her own first husband was frequently out of town. But it didn't matter now, Joanne told herself.

Liz advised Joanne in a friendly tone. "Derek certainly had a large estate, even by Sewickley standards."

"Yes. I probably shouldn't have divorced him actually."

Liz put on her glasses and handled the faxed documents. "Joanne, I don't think you will be happy with his instructions."

"In what way?"

"Well he left a large sum, $980,000 to the Sierra Club."

"That doesn't surprise me at all."

"And he left over a million dollars to Carnegie Mellon."

"Yes."

"And nearly a million to various charities, mostly in Becky's name or anonymously."

"OK. I can live with that."

"And $58,000 to some woman in Erie."

Joanne said nothing. She chewed on a piece of lettuce.

"And 14.7 million to Emily."

Joanne looked up. "Is that everything?"

"No. He left you $980 with a strict stipulation."

Joanne said nothing. Her facial expression turned dour.

Liz continued. "He must of promised you he would fix your garaged door opener."

"Yeah, he's been promising me that ever since he left."

Liz took a sip of her diet coke. "Well he is keeping his promise."

Joanne was visibly angry. It was probably better that she did not raise her voice because the elderly women across the room would be offended by her language. Liz sensed Joanne's frustration and reviewed her options.

"Of course we could file and contest this will."

Joanne looked at her.

"I think we would have a number of legal options. After all you are his former spouse, and the mother of his two daughters, one deceased. I think the court may want to hear that."

Joanne looked up. She thought for a moment that she would correct Liz but she did not. She queried.

"What about the life insurance? I was the beneficiary on his policy. I remember that."

"Yes. He had a whole life policy in the amount of five million dollars. And you are the only beneficiary."

Joanne sighed. Her shoulders relaxed ever so slightly. Liz continued. "But the usual procedure in a suicide case is for the insurance company to contest the benefit. I will have to look over the contract."

Joanne looked anxious again. Liz was uncomfortable with the subject but felt she needed to be straightforward. "I know Emily has been missing now nearly a week. Like you I pray for her safe return, but if anything were to happen to her you would likely have a strong legal claim to the fifteen million dollars Derek left her."

An uncomfortable period of time passed before Joanne looked up and met Elizabeth's eyes. They were different eyes from what the attorney expected to see. The look of her client frightened her although she gave no signal of distress. Joanne maintained her stare for slightly longer than was natural and then looked away. She stirred her clam chowder with her spoon and placed it on her salad plate.

Chapter 37

Nicki, with the help of a number of friends on campus, arranged activities to mark the one week anniversary of Emily's disappearance.   In creative writing class a framed picture of her with the caption "You are not forgotten." was placed in Emily's usual seat. There were yellow ribbons around the trees and students and faculty wore yellow armbands. At noon a special service was held in the Mary Herman Chapel and later a walk at Price Island Park was organized to raise money for an award for information leading to Emily's return.   The students had raised eight hundred and five dollars by afternoon.

Officer Richardson, the man in charge of the investigation for the Erie County Sheriff's Department, had run short on leads. He had met with young Sarah and Adam but he viewed their story as fanciful. They told him about the note and the cat but they couldn't produce either. He spoke with Adam's teacher and she told him that Adam had been known to invent a story now and then.   Richardson felt comfortable dismissing the information although he wondered the marital status of the teacher.

The policeman followed up on a report from a few locals that while staying at the homeless shelter on Peach Street an individual claimed to have slept with a number of local college girls. It seemed odd enough that he decided to take a drive downtown. He found none of the individuals in question at the shelter but had more success at the City Mission.

A thin African-American man named Luke sat at his table and ate soup and crackers. He had a slight tremor and appeared anxious. He wore his outdoor jacket at the table and had a United States Flag pinned to his lapel. He was missing some teeth. Officer Richardson sat across from him and laid his overcoat on the bench nearby.

"What was this guy's name?"

"Jim, or James, or Jimmy" Luke answered. He did not stop eating his soup.

"Did he have a last name?"

"If he did I didn't hear it?"

"Did he say anything else that concerned you?"

"Well, he threatened me." There was some soup on Luke's cheek. The officer said nothing. Luke continued.

"This is the Erie homeless shelter I told him. You shouldn't be coming in here."

"He isn't from Erie?"

"No. Buffalo." Luke savored his coffee in a white styrofoam cup. He waited for the officer's next question. He had been in trouble with the law himself in the past but nothing serious as he saw it, just being black in a white city. Anyway, he didn't sense any danger from this cop.

"Buffalo?"

"That's what I said. I told him that Buffalo's got shelters and that he should find a bed up there."

The officer looked at the homeless man. Luke continued to sip his soup and tell his story.

"Well he told me that he had killed before and that he could easily kill again. Then he lay down next to me and went to sleep. Of course after hearing that I didn't rest too well."

The officer did not give a look of sympathy nor did he thank him for the information. On way out he grabbed a few crackers from the bin and put them in his pocket.

Fuentes was back at the building adjacent to the Arnold Boat Yard. She had replaced the batteries in the surveillance camera and repositioned it. The camera appeared to be working properly. Even though her work at this vantage was complete something told her to sit. Something told her to wait. She checked her watch. She noticed the red light blinking on the camera body. She checked her watch again. It was dark now and a small light above the entrance to the Boatyard came on. Maybe there were a few flakes of snow falling. It had become colder. She checked her watch again.

With a sigh Fuentes stood to leave. She was getting stiff and there had been no activity at the boatyard. Then she saw the lights of a vehicle. They were bright and then off. It was a van. She watched as a middle aged man exited and walked to the metal door and entered the building. Fuentes moved away from the window so she would not be seen. At that moment she knew she needed to follow him into the building. She tried to quiet her racing heart.

Outside it was quite cold. She made her way across the snowy embankment and through the gravel lot behind the building. She walked up the stairs and knocked on the door, first in a normal manner, then quite loudly.   There was no answer. Then she remembered the metal shovel and the crowbar. She walked back to retrieve them and decided that one way or another she would enter the building.

Chapter 38

Fred Murtins briefly sat at his upstairs desk and completed an invoice. He had a number of phone messages but they could wait. He had two new girls to try out and since he started the antibiotics his penis felt much better.   He grabbed three rubbermaid containers from the stack in the corner by his workbench. He figured it was about time he got rid of the girl from Price Island Park. She was no good to him anymore. She should be dead by now or at least near dead. He would cut her up and load her into his van. Then he could drive up to his New York land tomorrow and leave her with the others. There was a lot of work involved in his hobby he told himself, but in the end it was worth it. After all he had never slept with a doctor before. He was looking forward to that. He put the containers on a dolly, opened the freight elevator and headed down.

The girl from Muddy River that he picked up a few days earlier looked absolutely terrified when he appeared.   She pleaded with him not to harm her and to let her go.   She fought him with all of her strength until he hit her with a club as she tried to pull away. She could only move so far with her leg chained to the cold floor like an animal. Murtins found the resistance amusing. He actually enjoyed subduing her. He strapped her to his dolly the way that he usually did and wheeled her to the secretary's room.

The medical student lay perfectly still listening carefully to all the activities nearby and tried to think of a way out. She was not able to see what was happening but knew precisely every move her captor was making. She feared that she would be next. Emily lay in her room motionless. If she was alive it was a wisp of life, like a low flame of a candle when the wick is nearly gone.

After Murtins finished with the girl from Muddy River he wheeled her back to her room, clamped the chain around her leg, and whacked her with his club for good measure. Then he moved to Emily's room. He was able to position her on his dolly without any resistance. She lay on the wooden cart flaccid and expressionless. Her eyes were open but looked like dull mirrors. Murtins noted the number "23" that he had burned into her back and again on each side of her buttock. The redness had subsided and was replaced with a waxy grey. He wheeled her into the secretary's room and looked for his circular saw.

Fuentes was at the door by the loading dock with the shovel and the crowbar. She positioned the blade of the shovel in the gap of the door and tried to pry it open. She rocked back and forth using the crowbar for leverage until the shaft of the shovel nearly split. No luck. Then she put the crowbar through the handle of the shovel and down across the blade to fortify it, and with the tip of the shovel in the crack of the door she was able to get it open enough that she was able to slip the crowbar inside. Then rocking back and forth for some time she was able to get near the dead bolt, reposition the crowbar and the shovel and rock on the dead bolt until it broke free. She could feel the sweat dripping down her back and she was breathing deeply so she crouched for a moment to regain her bearings. Then she entered.

Chapter 39

Doci had been asleep for over two hours but something startled her. She looked around her dark room, checked her husband who was quietly snoring, and glanced toward the window. Everything seemed still. It was not unusual for Marta to be out. She was often out late with work or other activities. Doci understood that Marta was an adult and had her own life. But something had startled her and now she felt uncomfortable. She took a walk to the bathroom. She washed her face with cold water and she crawled back into bed. Pa grumbled slightly, turned, and seemed to go back to sleep. Doci couldn't relax. She had a funny feeling in her chest.

Outside it was a cold February night. There wasn't much traffic on the road, only the occasional thrown light of a car in the curtains. The wind was quiet and the room was warm. Pa liked to keep the house warm. It helped with his diabetes. Doci lay in the bed with her eyes open. She had a feeling in her chest like butterflies and she prayed. Something wasn't right. So she prayed some more.

Marta Fuentes entered the large boat storage facility on the first floor of the Arnold Boathouse. The room was dark except for a light over a desk in the far corner and a red "Exit" sign beyond it. There were a number of boats on jacks covered with blue shrink wrap and there was a wall with a number of outboard engines in various states of repair. The building had an odor that did not belong to boat repair. It troubled Fuentes. With her flashlight in one hand and her other hand on her gun she moved into the dark space.

In the distance Fuentes heard faintly the muffled noise of an electric saw and she moved toward it. As she moved past the desk and the work area and toward the red "Exit" sign the noise, although muffled, became louder. She saw that there was a dark hallway and as she shined her light she could see that it ended in an elevator. She hesitated for a moment and then moved down the hall. She entered the elevator and saw that it could only go down one floor. There were no other options. She pushed the button "B" and felt the door close. Almost immediately the elevator motor rumbled and shook and she felt herself slowly moving down. At the same time she heard the electric saw shut off as if someone below had become aware of her presence. He was waiting for her. The former Erie County Sheriff's Deputy had no idea what she was about to encounter next. No amount of wartime duty nor training in law enforcement had prepared her for what was coming. The elevator clanked to a stop and with a mechanical sound the doors slowly opened.

Chapter 40

The first thing that hit Fuentes was the smell. The putrid waft of human feces, urine, and vomit struck her like a punch to the ribs. She gasped for air. Then for a moment she doubted her eyes. There was Murtins holding a circular saw in his right hand. Emily Verada, or what was left of her, lay motionless on a makeshift wheeled table. Murtins looked surprised as he looked up at Fuentes. Emily was waxy pale, naked, and perfectly still on the table.

Fuentes yelled at the top of her lungs. "Police Officer, Freeze!" She pointed her gun at the man.

Murtins looked at her smiling smugly.

"Drop the saw! Put your hands in the air!"

Emily lay between Fuentes and Murtins. If she took a shot at him, even at close range, she risked hitting Emily. Fuentes heard the cries of the other girls. She yelled out to them.

"I am a police officer. You will be rescued!"

There was loud crying from the other rooms. Murtins studied Fuentes and his situation. He moved more carefully behind Emily Verada. He did not appear frightened.

The medical student yelled out from her room. "Please be careful! He is a monster!"

Fuentes commanded. "Get down on the floor! Get down on the floor, you bastard. Let me see your hands."

Murtins moved slowly to his left. And then he seemed to look about the room and in an instant he exploded to the wall and flipped off the light. Total darkness enveloped the secretary's room and the hallway. The medical student screamed and Fuentes reached for her flashlight. There was a loud explosion and then a second and then Fuentes returned fire into the darkness. Fuentes felt her breath leave her and then she needed to cough and a foamy red substance came up. Suddenly she felt weak and confused. She sensed he was coming toward her so she fired again. He limped down the hall and the door slammed behind him. It was very quiet until the medical student cried out.

"Officer, are you OK?"

Marta was in and out of consciousness. She sensed she had been hit in the chest. Where was her vest, she wondered? She needed help. She dialed her cell phone. One ring.

"911 Operator. What is your emergency?"

"Police Officer Shot. Arnold Boat Yard. Need help immediately!"

"This is the 911 Operator. I am sorry I can not hear you. We must have a bad connection. Can you move to a better location? Hello, 911 Operator."

Fuentes crawled back into the elevator. She tried to stand but was not able. She touched her hand to her chest and became aware of the warm, wet covering of blood. She somehow reached her leg up the wall of the elevator and kicked the control panel until the door closed and the elevator rumbled up on flight. On the main floor she rested for a few seconds and dialed the blood covered cell phone again.

"911 Operator. What is your emergency?"

Fuentes struggled to whisper. She was rapidly losing her hold on life.

"Officer down. Arnold Boat Yard. Ambulance."

The 911 Operator paused. Fuentes could hear her making dispatch instructions in the background. She was contacting Police, Fire, and Paramedics. Then the 911 Operator returned to Officer Marta Fuentes and spoke.

"Officer, I am sending help. Hang in there. Help will be there shortly. Please stay on the line."

As she spoke Marta sensed the phone slipping from her warm, wet hand. She had an awareness that she may have cracked the case and she felt good about that. Except for the chest wound she had suffered it was a good day, she told herself. A very good day. Her breathing had become very shallow. At that moment the last drop her alertness slipped away.

Chapter 41

Within five minutes the Arnold Boatyard property was lit like a christmas tree. Various divisions of fire, rescue, and police moved in. On their heels the media moved from the Saint Veronica's Hospital Parking Lot to just beyond the perimeter. At least two Medivac helicopters landed by the rear garage door and another hovered above.

The information flow was chaotic and confused. The national media released unconfirmed reports that Fuentes and Verada were dead, and that Fred Murtins, a park ranger, was in custody. Later, they had to retract parts of everything that they rushed to get out. Actually the local media, with their sources within police, fire, and the nearby hospitals, was getting the story quickly and mostly correct.

A second perimeter was set up at the Murtin's residence, not too far away. He had apparently been wounded and had been bleeding severely as a trail of crimson led from his dark van into the residence and then out again. His blood stain on the white snow was unmistakable. His wife and son were home and appeared frightened. They were not talking. Murtins was gone. An "All Points Bulletin" was issued. His picture was posted on local and national broadcasts.

Officer Richardson and the others stood by the pool of blood where Marta Fuentes lay and shook their heads. She had been transported by helicopter to Harness Medical Center just 5 miles away and had been taken directly to Operating Room 6. Her condition was believed to be critical. Richardson lit up a cigarette and turned to one of the crime scene photographers.

"Did you see her before she left?" he queried.

The photographer looked up at him. "Yes sir, I did. They moved her pretty quickly, though."

"How did she look? Could you tell?"

"She looked bad, man. She looked really bad."

Richardson inhaled from his cigarette deeply and dropped it onto the bloody floor.

"Bastard!" He said.

The photographer nodded.

In the Emergency Room at Harness Medical Center Emily Verada arrived in full cardiopulmonary arrest. She was intubated and chest compressions were being done by the paramedic. She was hastily moved from the ambulance gurney to the table in trauma bay 3. The emergency room was otherwise busy and her arrival with fire, police, and the media created a circus atmosphere.

"I have no pulse." The intern advised.

"I am not getting a pressure." The nurse responded.

Both looked at the monitor which showed an agonal heart rhythm, not compatible with life.

Emily Verada lay naked, emaciated, and unresponsive as the emergency room team worked vigorously to resuscitate her with intravenous potions and electroshock to no avail. After some time the intern stood at the head of the bed and said.

"OK, let's call it off. She is not responding."

The others looked up. One of the nurses spoke quietly but forcefully.

"Doctor, I agree with you that it is probably hopeless, but shouldn't we have your attending come in here to pronounce this young lady? After all, this case is going to be looked at by a lot of people. You can count on that."

The intern looked at her, slightly angered. He paused for a moment before he spoke.

"OK, we can do that. I don't have any problem with that."

By now the media was hearing whispers that Emily did not make it. A respiratory therapist had whispered to her coworker that she was "dead as a doornail". Somehow that conversation got out to the waiting crowd. The phrase stuck with many of the reporters outside, although it would never show up in any story. Some of the reporters who had followed the story since the beginning and many of Emily's friends and supporters were hearing the murmurs of the crowd and were crying, some uncontrollably. Joanne Verada had not arrived yet, but had received the call to come immediately, and she was on her way.

Doctor McGee, the senior attending emergency physician on the unit that evening pulled back the curtain and moved to the bedside. He could see that all the protocols had been followed and he had a grim look on his face. He turned to the nurse who had asked for him and queried.

"What's her rectal temp?"

In the chaos to rapidly resuscitate they hadn't checked a temperature. The nurse rolled Emily on her side and quickly obtained the vital sign. She looked at the digital readout and tried again.

"79 degrees fahrenheit, if you can believe that?"

The attending seemed to gain a spark of hope. He turned to his intern and scolded. "She is as cold as a snowball. You can't ever pronounce someone until you bring their core temperature to normal. Slowly warm her up and keep resuscitating her."

"Yes sir." he answered impishly. The nurse made no expression of victory, whatsoever. She got the warming blankets and the intravenous warmers.

Within fifteen minutes Emily Verada was in a weak sinus bradycardia. Her core temperature was moderating and she developed a low, but measurable blood pressure that was being augmented by medication. By now the Intensive Care team from upstairs had arrived and was managing her care. One of the physicians for the I.C.U. turned to the nurse who had saved her life and spoke.

"She is on very thin ice, but we will take her upstairs and cross our fingers. Sound OK?"

The nurse looked him in the eye and smiled. "Thin ice, crossed fingers, and a warm bed in your unit is the best news she has had in a week."

As the intensive care doctor pushed the stretcher into the hall he turned to thank the emergency room crew but the nurse spoke first.

"Take good care of her, doctor."

He smiled, nodded, and rolled the stretcher with its attached IV poles and monitors into the large elevator that would take his precious cargo to the intensive care unit.

Chapter 42

Doci and Pa waited in a very small, warm room with a green couch separate from the usual visitor's area near entrance to the operating room. A social worker opened the door and checked on them periodically, but had no news to report. The hospital arranged for clergy to come in, but the priest was at a dinner party and would be delayed. There was steam heat coming from a vent across the room. It was very hot. There was a tall, narrow window that almost came to the floor. It wasn't the kind that a visitor could open. Outside it was snowing heavily, and ice and condensation blocked any view. There was the noise of the steam heat and of a clock ticking. Otherwise the room was silent.

After a long time a doctor poked his head inside the door to this waiting room, but when Doci and Pa looked up he said that he was sorry and closed the door. He wore surgical scrubs, a paper hat, and had a paper mask hanging from his neck. In the moment that Doci glanced at him she noticed that he was perspiring heavily and he looked frightened. A few minutes later the doctor returned with a nurse, a social worker, and a Catholic priest. They all introduced themselves and sat nervously on the green vinyl couch.

The doctor spoke first but he spoke quickly and nervously and Doci was not sure what he was saying.

"Is she in surgery?" she asked.

The nurse sat next to Doci and placed her hand over hers and spoke more clearly. "They took Marta to surgery and did their best but she did not make it."

She paused and was quiet. Doci started to cry. First softly and then much louder. Pa had not heard what the others had said but he saw Doci crying and knew what had happened. He spoke with a lisp. "Oh my god. Oh my god."

Pa then cried uncontrollably. The doctor looked anxious but he and the others waited for a long time before they left. At the end of the evening the social worker took Doci and Pa to a cab that waited by a rear entrance to the hospital. She gave them her card with her cell number and told them to call with any questions. The cab driver did not seem bothered by the amount of snow and ice on the roads and he was quite talkative. Doci and Pa said nothing. When they arrived at their home in Millcreek Doci opened her purse but the cab driver explained that the fare had been paid by the hospital.

Inside the house felt quite empty. Pa sat in his chair for a while and Doci fiddled with a teapot. Later, when they went to bed Pa prayed and weeped out loud in the darkness. Doci listened to him and said nothing. She couldn't stop the tears from running down her face. She looked outside at the snow falling in front of a street lamp and wondered what would happen next.

Chapter 43

Fred Murtins took his wife's Toyota Corolla and drove south out of town on back roads reasoning that the police were likely to set up a roadblock on the highway. When he got to Ellinbary, a town south of Erie he pulled onto Interstate 79 and headed south until he came to the rest stop and parked in a poorly lit area behind some semi trailers. He checked to make certain that mud and snow covered most of his license plate and he made his way to the public restroom.

He looked in the mirror and splashed cold water on his face. He had sustained a bullet wound to his left shoulder. He was bleeding heavily. He slipped into one of the stalls and took off his tee shirt and stuffed it into the wound. He was not able to lift his left arm at all. He put his wool shirt on again but did not put his left arm through the sleeve. He put his jacket on over his shirt and headed out.

In the parking lot he saw the flashing lights of a patrol car and three state troopers speaking with a number of the truckers. In the distance he could hear the drone of a helicopter. Murtins walked by innocently and said nothing. By the time he had returned to his car he noticed dark blood had already soaked the shoulder area of his jacket. He sat in his car and realized that he would need medical attention.

Certainly he couldn't return to any of the Erie hospitals he reasoned. They would be all over him. He remembered that there was a small hospital in Muddy River, some miles to the south. Maybe they would not connect him with the search, he thought. Maybe they would be out of touch with the regional news. He would let them stitch him up and them he could be on his way.

Murtins pulled out onto the highway and headed south into the snowy night. Not too long after he was underway he saw the red, blue, and orange flashing lights of the troopers coming up at a very fast pace. Murtins reached over to the glove box and pulled out his pistol and placed it in his lap. As the lights came closer his switched off the safety. The lights were on him and then in a flash passed and moved on down the highway. Murtins breathed a sigh of relief and headed to Muddy River.

Chapter 44

Emily Verada lay in ICU bed number three. By any measure she was clinging to life. She was receiving medications to control her heart rate and her blood pressure. Respirations were provided by a tube in her throat and mechanical ventilation. She was receiving powerful intravenous antibiotics and kidney dialysis was scheduled for the morning. She was cared for by one nurse who, despite the complexity of her care, found the time to rub her shoulders and hum to her.

For a while Joanne Verada had been at her bedside, but Emily was not alert, so after some time she and the others found a place to get some sleep. Nicki, her roommate from Mary Herman, slept in a chair by Emily's bed. The lights were turned down quite low in the ICU, but with many new admissions and a patient that was deteriorating, it was quite chaotic.

There were no windows in Emily's room and the outside seemed far away. At the end of the hall near the nurse's break room there was one tall window that the staff would go to occasionally to check on the weather. The snow continued lightly and the wind had picked up considerably so some of the flakes appeared to be falling skyward. From the window one could see the helicopters as they took off and landed on a lower roof.

In Emily's distant dream she found herself in a hotel room in Florida. She thought she could hear Nicki in the other room. She thought she could hear laughter. The laughter made her want to smile but something was in her mouth and she couldn't. As she tried to smile she found herself back in the secretary's room and he was coming down the hall. Emily was not able to identify what was happening as a dream. The smell was real. His footsteps were real. She could hear the other girl's screams but she could not help them. She was restrained. She felt a crushing tightness in her chest as he approached her. Her throat was parched and she couldn't scream. She couldn't scream for help. She was in a helpless terror.

The monitors at the nurses station for bed three began to alarm. First a low blood pressure and a slow heart rate, then a dangerously rapid heart rate. Her nurse was at her bedside. Was she having a seizure? She quickly gave her an intravenous sedative medication. She rubbed her neck and hummed until Emily was quiet again.

Chapter 45

It took quiet a while for the surgeon to arrive at the little hospital. He introduced himself as Dr. Wibet and squinted as he reviewed Murtins Xrays.

"Mr. Johnson, You have a nasty laceration and a comminuted fracture of your humerus. You say you shot yourself while cleaning your gun?"

Murtins, who had registered under the name of Fred Johnson replied. "That's right Doctor. Foolish of me, I know."

Murtins was receiving IV antibiotics and blood. He was given a consent form for surgery and an operating crew was called in.

"Do you have any family here with you?" Wibet asked.

"No. My wife and son are at home. She wants me to call after I get out of surgery."

Wibet seemed relieved. For some reason he didn't want to talk to Murtins' family.

"We will move you up to the operating room shortly. After surgery you will be taken to a room on the second floor. I guess you can call your family then."

Murtins smiled. Doctor Wibet moved in the direction of the door. He turned and to Murtins and finished. "As you may know Mr. Johnson since you were injured with a firearm we need to notify the police."

Murtins tried to remain calm and looked Wibet right in the eye as he lied to the doctor slowly. "Yes, doctor. The staff here has already notified them. I believe they are on route as we speak."

Wibet appeared relieved. He preferred not to call the police himself, but he would not say why. "That's great. I will see you in the operating room then, Mr. Johnson."

After a few minutes Murtins could see Doctor Wibet sitting at a formica desk brightly lit by florescent bulbs from above. They appeared to flicker as he wrote on yellow lined paper. He was sitting alone. When he finished writing he dropped his papers at a vacant clerk's desk and left his patient's view. Some time later a nurse with a pleasant smile came and rolled Murtins to the operating room.

The doors to the operating room closed with a rush of air and Murtins was given some medicine that gave him a pleasant feeling and after that everything was blank. Next he heard the moaning of a patient next to him and slowly came to wakefulness. He felt his arm in a tight bandage and held by a sling and a swath. The bandage felt dry. He could move his fingers. He noticed his jacket and clothes in a bag on top of a dresser in his room. There was a curtain that separated him from his moaning roommate. He could see out the window where a bright light illuminated the snow-covered parking area. One nurse walked the dimly lit hallway outside the room.

Chapter 46

Joanne and Nicki walked down a yellow lit hospital hall and arrived at a cafeteria that was closed with a cage like door that descended from above. Around the next bend there was a small room with various vending machines and a microwave on the counter. A cleaning woman sat in the far corner half asleep. Nicki and Joanne both purchased coffee from the machine, mixed in sweetener and cream and sat at a shiny table with locked chairs. The room had a faint odd odor and the lighting was harsh. Nicki looked at Joanne in the unflattering hue. She appeared to have aged materially since she had last looked at her closely.

"Tomorrow they will know if Emily will need a hip replacement."

Joanne sipped her coffee. "Yes, I guess that open wound caused a bad infection and it spread into the bone."

"I hope she doesn't need to get her hip replaced. She is too young for that."

Joanne nodded. Emily continued. "I have watched her run. She runs like a deer, so fast and effortless. You don't take the hip out of a deer. No way."

"Are they going to start the dialysis tomorrow?" Joanne asked.

"I think that is what the nurses said."

"Hopefully that will be temporary."

"Yes, hopefully."

There was a long quiet period while the two sipped their coffees. The cleaning woman stood up and looked confused. Then she smiled and left the area.

Joanne put down her coffee and spoke. "Boy, Emily got a lot of cards and flowers from the Mary Herman students. She will be happy to see them when she wakes up."

"We all love her. That's what you are seeing. The whole campus is praying for her. They want to see her well. And back at school."

Joanne smiled a half smile. The coffee was very bad. Nicki continued. "I may not be back on campus next year."

Joanne looked up. "What do you mean?"

Nicki continued. "Well, my dad lost his job at the accounting firm. Something about outsourcing or right sizing. Anyway, I have already hit my limit on my student loans and two credit cards, so it is kind of uncertain right now."

Joanne looked at her. "Oh, Nicki, I am sorry to hear that. Emily will be devastated if you are not her roommate senior year."

"Yes, I know. I feel the same way. I am hoping that something works out for my dad, but you know how the economy is."

"Yes, I know."

Nicki stirred her coffee with a wooden stick and continued. "Oh, and I forget to tell you how sorry I am that you lost your ex husband, I mean Emily's dad."

Joanne looked puzzled for a moment. "Oh, yes. Thank you, Nicki. It has been a tough few weeks."

Nicki nodded. The two sat under the bright lights in the otherwise empty hospital refreshment room. In the distance an elevator arrived, the door opened, and no one got on. There were footsteps outside but they were heading elsewhere. Nicki and Joanne sat with their coffees and were silent.

Chapter 46

The Critical Care Services Director joined the Emergency Room manager at the long table in the hospital administrator's office.   The manager held the chart of the patient who had registered as Mr. Fred Johnson of Ashtabula, Ohio. The secretary stuck her head in the door.

"He said he would be here by now.   He had an appointment with his proctologist this morning. I wouldn't ask him about it."

The two smiled and looked at their watches. When he did arrive he came in in a huff and quickly entered his bathroom and closed the door.   Sometime later the toilet flushed, he exited, and looked quite upset.

"What do you two want?"   He asked as he looked through the mail on his desk.

"We've got a problem, sir"

The administrator looked up.

The manager continued.   "Last evening a patient was admitted through the ER with a gunshot wound to the left arm and shoulder. He was taken to surgery and admitted to the floor."

"What's the problem? Did they cut off the wrong arm?" The administrative leader smiled at his own humor. The others looked at him respectfully. The manager continued.

"It turns out he may be the murderer that has been all over the news."

"Well that is a police issue." The administrator said authoritatively. "What did the cops say?"

The administrative director cleared her throat and spoke. "That is our problem. He has been a patient here for over twelve hours and we haven't notified law enforcement as of yet."

The expletives started to fly. The administrator's face turned red and he appeared to be breath holding. Finally he spoke. "All firearms injuries need to be reported to the police. That's the law you idiots. Even I know that. You haven't reported this to the state, have you?"

"No sir, we wanted to speak with you first."

The administrator was livid. He screamed out to his secretary. "Get me Betsy on the phone immediately." While he waited for her to dial the phone he grilled his managers.

"Which doctor was on in the ER?"

"One of the fill-ins."

"Who was the surgeon?"

"Wibet."

The secretary entered the room and relayed the message. "Betsy is out until two o'clock. She is getting her hair frosted. Did you want to talk to any of the other attorneys."

The administrator was angrier by the minute. "No, tell her to call me when she gets back." Then he turned to the other two.

"I don't want the board of health or any of those state people involved in this, do you understand?"

"But sir, isn't this a reportable adverse event."

"Let's let Betsy handle the state when she gets back. Can you change the record to show he arrived later?"

"No, because he went to surgery and they have their own records."

"Where is he now?"

"Second North."

"Who do you know at city police?"

The manager's eyes lit slightly. "I know Jeff Pollister. He used to date my daughter after his divorce. He might do me a favor. Let me call Jeff. I could tell him that the patient was unstable and came out of surgery very late and that we didn't want to disturb him."

The administrator looked at his managers angrily and barked instructions. "Call Pollistor right now and see if he will cut you a break. In the meantime go up to this patient's room and stand by his door and don't let him leave. Do you understand?"

The two nodded sheepishly. The administrator continued. "And don't call the state or anyone else until I have had a chance to talk to Betsy."

The managers left the administrator's office and climbed the back stairs to Second North. Both had worked as floor nurses in their earlier years and knew their way around the building quite well.　When they arrived at the nurse's station the ward clerk and the charge nurse knew something was up.

"Do you have a patient, Fred Johnson?"

The charge nurse answered. "Room 213, bed 2."

The director's breathed a sigh of relief and walked briskly to the patient's location.　In the room they found a cleaning person wiping down the bed rails.　The morning sun was shining in the window and she was taking pride in her work.

"Where is Fred Johnson?"　The ER Manager barked.

The cleaning lady looked up but did not stop wiping the disinfectant on the bed rails when she spoke.

"He's gone.　He left during the night.　I saw him walk out the back stairs. I was concerned because he didn't have a jacket and it was quite cold here in Muddy River last evening.　I hope he is all right."

Chapter 48

The funeral for Officer Marta Fuentes couldn't have come on a colder day. Pa and Doci were huddled from the church to one of the lead cars for the long procession across the snowy city to the burial site. The cold and ice were not the problem, it was the biting wind that came from the north and west and across the lake. Hundreds of officers from across Pennsylvania and surrounding states came to show support. The governor had planned to attend but weather blocked his trip. There was no mention that Marta had been laid off just days before she was murdered. There was no mention that the chest wounds she suffered may have been prevented if she had been wearing her ballistic vest, a piece of equipment she had turned in when she left the department. There was no mention that Doci and Pa would not receive any of the benefits accorded to the beneficiaries of working officers; a death payment, a designated pension assignment, health care coverage, and the like.

Pa's blood sugars had been dangerously out of control since Marta's death. He had no appetite, and he couldn't seem to regulate his diabetes.

"I better stay in the car." he said to Doci.

"Yes, I think that would be best." she replied.

"Do you think they will be long?" he asked.

"No, I think they will say a few prayers and then everyone will want to get over to the church hall. I hope you will feel like eating something."

"Yes, I hope so." Pa replied.

Pa was holding Doci's hand as the black Cadillac pulled into the cemetery. The procession snaked around for what seemed like a long time and Doci could see the train of vehicles behind with their flags headlights on. They seemed to go on for a long time until they were out of sight in the blowing snow. When the car finally stopped the driver opened the door on Doci's side and cold air rushed in.

Doci thanked the driver and indicated that Pa would be staying in the car. As she got out he mumbled something and she turned to him with a kind, pale, purple-tinged face.

Pa cleared his throat and spoke softly. "Doci, tell her that I love her."

Doci smiled. "I will."

The driver took Doci's arm and the two walked forward into the snow and wind toward the grave site. As the others crowded around the priest began his remarks. To the many in the back it was not possible to hear his words. As he spoke he held his hat so it would not blow off. After he finished a shivering Doci kneeled in the snow right over the casket and crossed herself.   Then she stood, turned, and was wobbly. Many moved forward to assist her.

The driver took Doci's arm again and the two walked back to the car. She noticed little of the place, the other people, the rolling hills, the maze of small plowed roadways to the different sections of the cemetery. She didn't see how the snow sat on the northern part of the markers, blown from the wind and frozen in place. She didn't hear the winter birds in the leafless oak trees chirping loudly then diving down as groups and dispersing to smaller trees throughout the cemetery. She moved slowly and kept her eyes on the slippery path below. When the black car came into view she saw her husband. He wasn't looking outside the car. He didn't seem to see her. The driver opened the door and Doci stepped inside and took his hand.

Pa turned to Doci and asked. "How did it go?"

Doci squeezed a little tighter on his hand and answered. "Everything was fine."

In the western sky there was a bit of brightness. It was not sunshine. The black funeral car inched away causing the ice and frozen snow on the road to pop and crackle. It did not circle and left the cemetery. Doci and Pa did not look out. They were absolutely silent.

Chapter 49

On the fourth hospital day the breathing tube was removed from Emily's throat. She was moved to another room. It was quiet. The sheets were clean and the room was warm. There was a lightness in her throat and on her chest. Across the room was a window and through an open space in the curtains she could see light from the outside. There were many plants and stuffed animals on the dresser and the window sill. They had tags with messages of love and good wishes for her. She could not see any of that from her bed. Emily had pain in the open wound on her hip were the surgeons had debrided the infected tissue. She was hooked up to an intravenous line that was bandaged around her right forearm.

Emily felt frightened. Before her kidnapping, rape, and torture she almost always felt excited about her day. Now she was awake and warm but the room didn't feel safe. She was in a new place. It was clean, but it felt uncertain. Would someone come in and attack her, she wondered? The door opened directly to the hall. She wondered what was out there. She told herself not to be ridiculous, that this was a hospital and they were taking good care of her. She smiled inside at her foolish logic. She reached for her call button and paused. She wondered who was on the other end of that button. She put it down. She felt frightened. Maybe she would ask to be moved to another room. Yes, that would be a good idea she told herself.

Later in the day a family meeting had been scheduled. Emily's doctors, nurses, and social workers had planned to meet with Joanne and Nicki to discuss Emily's progress and their plan to transfer her to a rehabilitation facility. The timing was bad in that Nicki had an exam and Joanne was back in Sewickley on a personal matter. Emily's social worker sent out an email to everyone involved that it would be best to reschedule the meeting.

Emily spent most of the day in her room without visitors. She was unaware that some Mary Herman students had stopped by the nursing station but were turned away. She was unaware of the prayer service that was being held for her on campus everyday. She could not see the hundreds of flowers and well wishes that were left for her on a section of the hospital lawn or the yellow ribbons on thousands of trees in Erie and the surrounding areas. She would only learn of those things later.

Eventually the sliver of light between the curtains turned grey and then dark. Emily tried to sleep but she could not. She wanted to push the call button but waited. She heard some activity outside her door and her heart raced. Then whatever it was moved away. She moved her fingers and toes and told herself that everything would be OK. Then she remembered the smell of that place and what he did to the other girls. She wondered if maybe she would be safer in the intensive care unit with the breathing tube. Nobody was bothering her in there. Everything seemed better there. She reached for the nurse's button again and took a deep unsatisfying breath. She felt like she needed to get away but where would she go?

At some point Emily's racing thoughts calmed and she fell into a restless sleep. She had an awareness of her bandaged thigh and that the wound was draining and needed attention. She had an awareness of announcements that were being made over the public address system about visiting hours. In the confusion of her slumber she wondered who she was visiting in the hospital and why she hadn't left with the others. She told herself that as soon as she awakened she would need to find the other visitors and take the same elevator home.

Chapter 50

FBI agents pulled into the parking lot of a Scranton area used car dealer. The sign over the door read "Reliable Motors". It had been painted over a number of times but the lettering had faded in the harsh weather.   When the two officers entered the building a smiling salesman extended his hand and welcomed them.

"What can I do for you gentleman?"

His smile was not reciprocated. One of the plain-clothed agents showed the salesman the report of an title inquiry on an '06 Corolla believed to be owned by Murtin's wife.

"What can you tell me about this vehicle?"

The salesman's smile softened. "Gee, officer. I don't know anything about any small Toyotas. We mostly deal in domestics."

Another employee came from the back office. Both of the individuals looked nervous. The FBI man continued.

"We don't have time for any games. We know a title search on the vehicle was initiated at this location. Don't get yourself in any deeper trouble than you're already in."

The two men looked about evasively. The FBI men were quiet. Finally the older brother took out a cigarette, lit it, and spoke.

"This guy came by a few days ago wanting to sell us his car."

The agent interrupted. "Was he this man?

He showed the salesman a folded picture.

"Yes, that's him. He had his arm in a sling, however. That was definitely the guy."

The younger brother continued. "He told us that he was going to report the vehicle stolen. He said he needed $700."

"And you gave him the money?"

"No. We gave him $400."

"And where is the car?"

"Well, we ran a title search to see if we could sell the car on our lot. And when we saw that a lien was present we sold it to a parts broker in town."

"How does that work?"

"They just gave us $800 no questions asked."

"You realize you are dealing in stolen property, right?"

"Yes, officer. The economy is very bad. I have a family to feed. Of course it is wrong. I am very sorry."

The FBI agent looked at him sternly. "Where did Mr. Murtins go after you gave him $400."

"He asked us to drive him to the bus station in Scranton."

"And..."

"We did that, sir." The salesman looked at his brother and repeated. "We did that, sir."

At the bus station there were a number of people sitting on benches waiting for their connection. Duffle bags, suitcases, and backpacks lay along the wall and in the corner of the large room. There was the distinct smell of diesel fumes and old vomit inside. Occasionally a raspy voice came over the public address system and bleated departures and arrivals. From Scranton buses were leaving for just about everywhere. The two FBI agents looked out of place in their shiny black shoes, white shirts, and dark jackets. The station manager explained that they had put in surveillance cameras since the three murders four years ago. That, he told them, would be their best chance to find Murtins and to identify which bus he had left on.

Chapter 51

Bob LeClair of East Lake, Ohio stood outside the yellow crime tape on the small piece of land north of Findley Lake, New York. He watched the excavators dig through the snow-covered ground.   He wanted to know if his daughter Julie, missing now for three weeks, was buried in a shallow grave on this plot of land owned by Fred Murtins. The wind blew from the northwest and Bob's face turned red and blue from its bite.   He had been coming to the site everyday since the detectives had told them of their investigation.

Earlier in the week news crews from Erie, Pennsylvania and Jamestown, New York reported remotely from the site but when a frozen arm passed in view of the cameras a number of viewers complained to the stations that the report was too graphic. Apparently they preferred hearing more about the local school boards and the pie eating contests. One of the station managers in Erie concluded that the viewers wanted to put the gruesome events behind them and were tiring of the story. He decided only to report on positive developments such as Emily's progress with her recovery or if Murtins were to be captured. That didn't sit well with Bob LeClair at all. He couldn't let the story go.

One of the back hoe operators, a grizzled older man named Smythe, took his breaks with LeClair in Bob's truck. Smythe, despite the subtle disapproval of law enforcement, explained to LeClair the plan and results at every step of the way. The two had become friends in a way. Alternately, Smythe had become a counselor to LeClair. He encouraged him to come to the site. LeClair appreciated his efforts. There was no way that anyone would be able to tell in the field if his daughter Julie was among the frozen body parts. They were being retrieved covered in snow and ice and mud. They were quickly put in blue plastic bags and labeled, then taken by the Coroner's office. It would be days before identifications would be made. Nevertheless Bob LeClair felt it important to be there.

Julie had been his only daughter. She had been a championship tennis player, and after junior college, wanted to attend Princeton. She had no enemies. Her downfall was her attractiveness and the fact that she jogged by a boatyard in East Lake that Murtins occasionally visited. Unlike the others Deputy Sheriff Marta Fuentes had been hot on the trail of Julie's kidnapper. It had only been a matter of days since she died that Fuentes had broken up the whole thing. Unfortunately now both were gone. Bob LeClair exited his truck closing the door against the wind and cold firmly. He walked over to the edge of the crime tape and carefully watched the continuing excavation.

Chapter 52

Nicki pushed Emily in her wheelchair down the hall to an alcove at the end of her ward. Along with the chair she guided an IV pole on a rolling base and a machine that inflated stockings on Emily's legs.

"My doctors told me I might be discharged tomorrow." Emily confided.

"That's great news. Have you been able to stand, or walk?" Nicki queried.

"No, neither. Although they say my butt wound is healing good and maybe I won't need a hip replacement after all."

Nicki noticed how gaunt and dusky Emily appeared. She tried to remain positive. "Where are you going next?"

"They want to send me to a rehab hospital for about three weeks. I guess I have to build up my strength. You know, learn to stand and walk again."

"Of course. Where will that be?"

"Well mom wants me to go to Pittsburgh so it would be easier for her. Of course I would like to stay around Erie. That's where all my friends are."

Nicki nodded but said nothing.

"Nicki, would you come visit me at rehab if I stay in Erie?"

Nicki hugged Emily. She felt like a skeleton. "Of course I would, Emily. We all would. Everyone over at Mary Herman misses you so much. You know that."

"Good, then I hope I can stay in town."

They both were quiet for a long while. Nicki checked her phone and texted back a few messages. Emily let the sun shine through the window on her. It was warm. She felt almost safe.

"Nicki, I think I can get through all of this physical recovery stuff OK."

Nicki looked at Emily. She was a good listener. Emily continued. "But I wonder if I will ever feel like myself again."

Nicki queried. "What do you mean?"

"Well, ever since I have gotten out of that cage I have felt so anxious. Like something bad is just about to happen. I've been having terrible thoughts and frightening dreams. I can't make them stop. I am worried that I am going to be an emotional cripple."

Nicki thought for a minute before she replied. Then she spoke calmly and in a reassuring tone. "I'm sure that is normal after everything you have been through."

Emily smiled slightly. Nicki smiled back. Emily continued. "And I have flashbacks, I mean a sense that I am back there, and he is coming after me."

"Have you told your doctors about this?"

Emily smiled. "They are always in a hurry. Besides, they are working to get me physically well. You are the only person I have told."

Nicki started to wheel Emily back to her room. She didn't know exactly what to say to her. She couldn't imagine how terrible her experience had been. She tried to comfort her.

"I think in time some of the emotional stuff you are telling me will lessen, but I until then I will try to help you anyway I can."

When they got back to Emily's room the two girls hugged and Nicki left for the day. Emily did not want to be alone so she pushed the call button and a nurse's aid came and sat with until she drifted off into a nap. Later, when the social worker came in and told her that she had been placed in Erie and would not be going to Pittsburgh she felt mixed emotions about what the next phase of her recovery would bring.

Chapter 53

During the winter in Erie one snowstorm follows another. The snowbanks widen and the streets narrow. Runners are pushed off the trails and onto the road. The ice fisherman drill deeper to find water. Those who are bothered by the lack of sunshine feel less hopeful by the day. The abandoned mills, factories, and warehouses are covered in snow. Giant icicles hang from their roofs. There is no talk of leaving the place. The wind can bite hard.

The State Parks Department had hastily announced a press conference the day before. Six inches of lake effect snow fell over night at Price Island. The local reporters and TV crews were all there. Fred Murtins remained at large. There had been no updates on the case for days. The hospital had not allowed any access to Emily Verada. Even a few national correspondents tried to get to Erie but were stranded at the Pittsburgh awaiting flights to resume to Tom Ridge Field. There were rumors that the FBI might be present and answer some questions.

The access road to the park was covered with snow and ice. The conference was held at the Ranger Station at mile 2.2 on the multi-purpose trail. A number of men in dark suits and galoshes arrived carrying briefcases. The whisper was that they were lawyers from Harrisburg. At noon the room was packed and the small podium was flooded with white light. The room buzzed with anticipation.

"Maybe there is a breakthrough in the case." a reporter whispered.

At that moment one of the individuals came to the podium and addressed the crowd, almost instantly quiet with anticipation. Snow fell outside as he cleared his throat, and then he spoke.

"I am attorney Johnson Mathew, and on behalf of the Commonwealth of Pennsylvania, Department of Natural Resources, Parks, and Conservation I would like to make a statement. If there is time I will take a few questions."

He then introduced the team had had brought with him from Harrisburg, each standing then sitting, and then read from a pre-printed statement.

"Approximately three and half weeks ago a college student from Erie, Pennsylvania was allegedly abducted from this park and held until she was rescued by law enforcement. It is my understanding that the victim is recovering at a local hospital. The State Department of Natural Resources wishes the victim, Emily Verada, our best for a speedy recovery. Throughout this investigation the Park Service has fully cooperated with this ongoing investigation. One of the prime suspects in this case, Fred Murtins, of Millcreek, Pennsylvania remains at large as far as we know as of today. The press has reported that Mr. Murtins was an employee of the Price Island Parks Service at the time of the incident. We are here today to set the record straight with regard to Mr. Murtins. He was never a direct employee of the Parks Service as has been reported in the press."

The attorney could see the disappointed faces throughout the crowd. They had come to get new information on the case, but rather were given a legal statement that was a blatant attempt to reduce the Park's liability should a lawsuit arise. It didn't matter the attorney reminded himself. He had a job to do. And he did it well. He didn't ask if there were any questions. The crowd had started chaotically to ask them.

"What was Mr. Murtins' status then?"

"He was a contract employee. That is he was employed by a firm who provided services for the park, but not a direct employee of the park."

"Aren't we splitting hairs here? Did he wear a park uniform?"

The attorney pondered the answer. "Technically yes, but as I said Mr. Murtins was neither an employee of the Commonwealth of Pennsylvania nor the Price Island Park Service at the time of the alleged incident."

There was a gasp of disappointment in the room. Not only had there been no new information of this case, but now the suspect's putative employer was running from its relationship with him. It appeared sour to the people in the room.

"Do you have anything new to report on the case? Are we any closer to finding the suspect?"

The attorney looked confused, but answered. "That, I believe is a question for law enforcement."

The group dispersed as quickly as it formed. There were a few soft cackles from the media people as they left the room in groups and on cell phones. The legal team gathered in the corner and praised each other for a job well done. A few interested citizens left looking confused.   Outside the snow had tapered but the wind blew fiercely from across the lake.

Chapter 54

The transfer to the rehab facility was fraught with discomfort. The ambulance was late, and it had a leaky window that let in cold air. The facility, on the east side of town, was old and clean, but smelled strange to Emily. Joanne made the long drive from Sewickley. She waited in what would be Emily's room as the doctors and intake personnel made their assessments. Emily felt anxious and uncomfortable as the doctors thoroughly examined her. Blood was drawn and a nurse took a urine sample through a single use catheter. Emily was relieved when they were finished.

She was wheeled through an open area where cheerful therapists worked with severely disabled people and down a hall to a room with four beds. She was happy to see her mother waiting at her bedside. Joanne looked up and tried to be positive.

Emily spoke first. "Hi mom, I missed you."

"Hi sweetheart. You made it OK?"

Emily nodded. A nurse helped her to her bed.

Joanne couldn't resist. "I was hoping you would have been admitted closer to Sewickley, but this place seems fine."

"I know mom, but my school friends can come over here, and maybe I can have a tutor from Mary Herman."

"Well, that would be nice."

There was a long silence as Emily looked around her new surroundings. Her three roommates were off having treatments so the area was open. She let her head rest back on the pillow. It felt different from the one at the hospital.

Joanne spoke again. "I am not going to be able to come everyday dear. Since your father died I have been struggling financially."

Emily had learned of her father's suicide while she was in the hospital. She had not been told of her inheritance however. Her mother's comments slipped by her.

"Well, I hope you will come often..."

Before Emily could finish one of her doctors entered the room and introduced himself. Emily did not catch his name.

"Are you her mother?" He asked Joanne.

"Yes."

"Could I speak with you briefly?"

"Of course."

"No, I mean outside."

Joanne looked at Emily slightly surprised. What could he tell her that he wouldn't tell Emily.

"Certainly."

Joanne and the doctor walked out into a quiet part of the hall by a janitor's closet. Emily let her head sink into the pillow and began to drift off.

"I will be one of the physicians responsible for your daughter's care while she is our facility."

"OK, well I am glad to know you."

"We have examined your daughter and reviewed her hospital reports and want to get started on her rehabilitation right away."

"Yes, I think that is a good idea. And I believe Emily wants her life back as soon as possible."

The doctor paused before his next question, and he phrased it carefully.

"Is Emily aware of her condition?"

Joanne gave a confused expression. "Yes, I think so. What do you mean, doctor?"

"Well, we ran a pregnancy test today, as part of our intake, and Emily's result is positive."

Joanne let out a long gasp. The hospital had not thought to run a pregnancy test, or maybe they did and didn't tell them the result. Pregnant by a killer, then radiated and medicated with all kinds of risky therapies. That cannot be good Joanne told herself.

"We will have to terminate it immediately. Does Emily know?"

"That's what I wanted to ask you. That's why before I speak with her I wanted to talk to you."

Joanne looked at the doctor and confirmed. "Emily knows nothing about being pregnant. When you talk to her please convince her to end it right away. This is madness!"

The doctor put his hand on Joanne's shoulder. "I will do my best." He turned and walked to Emily's room holding a clipboard in a way that resembled a protective shield. After he entered the room. He closed the door and sat at her bedside.

Emily gave him a curious look and he started to share his information with her.

Chapter 55

Ten days into her rehab Emily was walking in the hall with a cane. Her mother had not been back since the first day. Nicki sat on her bed and typed on Emily's Ipad. It had been a gift from Emily's dad.

"Do you think you will be able to come back to school soon?" Nicki asked.

"That's the plan." Emily said with a smile. She was standing at the door to the hallway. The room was otherwise empty. The other patients were off at therapy.

Emily continued. "They are telling me I am way ahead of schedule with my physical therapy."

"That's good." Nicki smiled.

Emily continued. "But I still get terrible, vivid nightmares. Last night I woke up my roommates twice. And I have these spells, like panic spells, when I can't breath and feel like I need to run away."

"What do your doctors say?" Nicki asked.

"They seem to be ignoring it." Emily replied. "But that is what is bothering me the most. I want the flashbacks, dreams, and panic states to subside."

"What about your pregnancy?" Nicki asked.

"Nobody is talking about it. I guess they are hoping it will just go away."

"And your mom?"

"She is furious. She is giving me the silent treatment; no visits, no emails, no calls."

"Huh!" was Nicki's reply. She was always taught a family should stay together, no matter what the challenge. Even now with Nicki's dad out of work Nicki planned to do whatever her family needed, even if it meant putting college on hold.

"Well I am there for you, Emily. No matter what happens next."

Emily pushed herself with her cane and made it to her institutional bed and sat next to Nicki. She fought back the moisture that was forming in her eyes and gave Nicki a hug. It was a nice feeling to have someone express love that wasn't conditioned on something.

"Mom is even sending Father Murphy over from Mary Herman to see if he can convince me to get an abortion."

The two girls laughed.

"Father Murphy?"

"Yeah. Father Murphy. Maybe mom made a big donation to the college or something, but I heard he was coming to visit."

Nicki laughed as she checked the time. Father Murphy was the sweetest old man that she had ever met. He had given her an "A" in a course that she should not have passed, simply because she smiled a lot. She did not think him a persuasive man, however. A cheerful therapist stuck her head in the door and chirped at Emily. Nicki hugged her again and left.

Chapter 56

Three weeks into her rehab stay Emily was walking in the hall without her cane. Her thigh wound was healing well. There was no further talk of a hip replacement. Her discharge was ready for the following day although her mom had not been in in over a week and there were some uncertainties over the plan. Emily had voiced concerns with her nurse and doctors over what were now being called "panic attacks". These episodes seemed to appear out of nowhere and hit like a bolt of lightning. To Emily they were terrifying. In addition she was experiencing vivid flashbacks and having trouble sleeping. She continued to have terrible nightmares that were not diminishing and often she found herself having difficulty concentrating on the simplest of things. Her caregivers seemed to want to focus on her remarkable physical progress and slough off her psychologic complaints. In Emily's mind she always knew she would recover physically, but she felt shame for her emotional weakness. She secretly wished someone would acknowledge the real battle she faced. Maybe then she could get well, she told herself.

Father Murphy stood at the visitor's station in the front entrance of the building. He was a cheerful elderly man in full priest garb who looked lost, but cheerfully so. The volunteer at the front desk walked him to Emily's room and he stuck his head in with a smile. Emily knew Father Murphy well. He had been her English 104 teacher freshman year. He wasn't the best teacher, but he was kind and attentive, and wouldn't dare grade someone lower than a "B", so the students liked him. He could have retired years ago, but he was forthright with his friends and students. Where would he go?

"Hello, Father." Emily reached out her hand and walked him to a chair in the corner of the room. She sat on her bed.

"Well, Emily. I was expecting to see a sick person. You look grand. I have been praying for you everyday. God has asked a lot of you."

He had a faint Irish brogue. Emily knew why he was visiting. She knew what her mother put him up to. But she was polite. She let him proceed.

"Emily, I wonder if could speak with you about a delicate matter."

"You mean my pregnancy, Father."

"Yes."

There was a long pause, then a sigh, and then the kindly priest looked outside before speaking again. "Emily, in a circumstance such as this, in a crime, a hideous crime..."

The room was silent. The priest moved forward in his chair and continued. "I want you to know that the church can offer leniency to you should you decide..."

Emily's face was smooth and her eyes were clear. "Father, I am not requesting any leniency."

"No. No, you are not. But you are a young, unmarried woman. You have a bright future ahead of you. A pregnancy under these circumstances might complicate things for you."

"Tell me about it, Father"

They both laughed. The priest continued. "I want you to know that under these particulars you have options. I want you to at least think about what I am saying. I know you have been through a lot. I can't even imagine."

"Yes, Thank you Father."

"And we can't wait until you are back at Mary Herman. We all miss you terribly."

Emily smiled. "Did my mom send you?"

Father Murphy thought for a moment. "We did talk on the phone. Your mother is terribly upset. She wants you to reconsider."

Emily sighed. "I wish she could be more supportive. I know I have made the right decision. But now I feel alone."

Father Murphy smiled and said nothing. He knew what it was like to feel alone. He smiled again and didn't force the issue. The conversation moved to all the campus activities that Emily had missed, the big snowman that someone had built outside her dorm, and the excitement that was building for her return. For a moment things almost felt real for Emily, as if the inner fear that was now her constant companion had left. She felt a tinge of excitement, of happiness, but she wondered if she could trust that feeling. It was a very nice moment for her to have. Outside the snow had melted on the west lawn of the rehab facility. A robin perched near her window. The breeze seemed a bit milder and the sun, although faint, seemed higher in the sky. At that moment Emily knew she was ready to leave the rehab facility. Speaking with Father Murphy had convinced her of that. She watched as he walked slowly down the hall and out the front door, turning to smile and wave as he did.

Chapter 57

The FBI had formed a task force that was internally known as "Price Island". Fred Murtins had been placed on the list of "10 most wanted suspects". There was a website with photos and an address to leave tips anonymously. The national TV show "America's Most Criminal" was preparing a piece on Murtins to air in an upcoming broadcast. As a result the task force had received over six thousand tips and followed up on almost twelve hundred. They appeared no closer to an arrest.

Bob LeClair, father of Julie, "victim 22" as they were now calling her, followed the activity of the task force obsessively. When a civil liberties blog out of a California law school reported that the interrogation of Murtin's wife had been particularly harsh LeClair fired off a powerfully worded criticism to the University President reminding him that this case was not someone's theory, rather that his own daughter had been captured, raped, and killed by a man who remained at large.

A few days later LeClair's letter was published in the University Daily Paper as part of a favorable story and the University President called him personally to be sympathetic. About a week later the bloggers wrote another piece acknowledging the tragedy, but indicated that Murtin's wife was not a criminal. They believed that the evidence showed that she had not known of her husband's activity and had not been accused of or charged with any crime. Given these facts, they reiterated that she should be treated the way any other witness is treated, with dignity and respect. LeClair had no real issue with the wife of this monster, and he felt a morsel of pride that he was able to move the needle ever so slightly at a university he probably couldn't locate on a map. He wanted Murtins captured and brought to justice. No bloggers were arguing fair treatment when his only daughter was chained to the floor, raped daily, and starved to death.

The FBI followed leads that led to one eyed men from Tacoma to Winter Haven. They pulled teachers from their classrooms, drivers from their trucks, and drifters from their places of hiding. Some of these individuals had sordid pasts on their own and answered questions nervously, but in the end none were linked to the parks and boatyards of Erie, Pennsylvania. Although frustrating the task force maintained the attitude that every unhelpful lead was simply one lead closer to a breakthrough.

Since Murtins had links to a pre-Soviet Russia there was a theory that he had returned to the Ukraine. This is why his wife and friends had been questioned so voraciously. They would be likely to know, the task force reasoned, if he had fled the country. It would be relatively easy for someone from Erie with boating expertise to make his way quietly into Canada undetected. Once in Canada he could travel cross country to Alaska and across the Bering Sea into Russia. His wife related that both she and her husband spoke fluent Ukrainian, and that they had friends and family in that region.

With these theories in mind the task force worked closely with the Canadian authorities on all matters of the investigation. Working with the former Soviet states was a trickier matter, but diplomatic channels were explored. If Murtins had escaped to the Ukraine U.S. authorities recognized that they would have to pay up for information leading to his location and capture. Officially they would not speak of these things, but on all fronts they were willing to entertain any manner of compensation for the information. As one unnamed official put it off the record. "We may have secret prisons full of international prisoners just for these occasions. We have lots of options when it comes to trading for information."

The Canadians were prompt, helpful, and good partners in all regards when working with the task force. The Ukrainians did not want this monster walking their soil any more than the Americans, but it was in their "DNA" to try to get something if they were going to give something. So to the delight of some elderly mid-level Soviet bureaucrats who missed the cold war days the U.S. State Department rolled out the proverbial "red" carpet and asked for their help.

Almost all of this investigative activity was going on out of the public eye. To those who were following the case it appeared that little was being accomplished. Certainly no breaks in the case were being reported. The press was hungry for information, and when none was forthcoming, the tone of some of the stories turned to "why isn't more being done?". Almost everyone had a theory about where Murtins was. On a cold and blustery day of March, weeks after his daughter's savagely dismembered body was identified on Murtins upstate New York land, Bob LeClair logged onto the internet and searched for any new information or commentary on the case. There was nothing.

Chapter 58

When Pa fell to the floor Doci was not surprised. She bent over to arouse him and when he didn't respond she moved quickly to the kitchen and dialed the black rotary phone. It seemed funny in a way to her. They had been together for sixty-three years. She had rehearsed this moment in her mind many times but now it had a dreamlike feel. It was not what she would have imagined. She gave her address to the woman on the 911 desk and she sat in the chair by the window and waited for the ambulance to arrive.

Everything seemed distant to Doci. She could hear the sirens far away getting louder. She knew that Pa had not been himself since they buried Marta. The last few evenings he had been restless in bed and the last night she knew he didn't sleep at all. His color had been poor and he was not eating anything. Lately he seemed more confused than usual. Doci sat in the chair and watched Pa. He was still. In the background the mechanical clock that they had received as a gift many years earlier ticked and tocked. Otherwise it was quiet.

When the paramedics arrived there was a pounding on the door and a lot of commotion. They had Pa on his back and they were putting needles in his arms and a plastic tube in his throat. He seemed to be fighting them aimlessly. Doci was told the name of the hospital and was advised to take a cab or ride in with a neighbor. Her sense was that this time it was not good for Pa.

After everyone left Doci went to the her bedroom. She changed out of her bathrobe into a dress and put on some shoes. She grabbed her rosary beads, looked at the faded black and white picture of her and Pa from before they were married, and she touched it as she said a prayer out loud. The neighbor was happy to help and Doci, the neighbor, and her young daughter rode quietly to downtown Erie to the hospital.

At the information desk a young lady hustled Doci into a small room by the Emergency Room. It had a couch, a few chairs, an end table with a lamp, and some paintings hanging behind glass. The woman left Doci in the room, smiled and closed the door all but a crack as she left. The neighbor had taken her daughter to find the restroom and to get her a candy bar. Doci sat alone. She imaged other people ushered into the this room, maybe every day.

Doci knew what was coming. But she could only describe her emotions as numb. Sixty-three years is a long time to be with someone. Sixty-seven if you count the time before they were married. It had been a good partnership she told herself. They had had a lot of fun, especially in the early days. When Pa got sick things slowed down, but when Marta came to stay their was great happiness again. Doci remembered a time when she and Pa drove up to Niagara Falls when they had first gotten married. It wasn't their honeymoon, that was months before. There was an argument over something and it felt serious. She tried to remember what the fight was about, but was unable to recall. As a result they left early and were silent the entire trip home. Doci told herself that regardless of who caused the spat she was in the marriage for the long haul and that when they got home and Pa had cooled off she would apologize. When they did get home something came up and a day or two passed, and things were back to their usual routine. Now sixty-three years later it burdened her. She wanted to say she was sorry.

There was some muffled talking outside the door and then a doctor, nurse, and a priest entered and sat on the couch. Before anyone said anything Doci remembered that she had forgotten to fill the bird feeder with black sunflowers and that she had left a quart of skim milk out on the kitchen counter. She wondered what kind of candy the little neighbor girl liked. She had always liked chocolate-covered raisins when she was small, and if she had been good her father would take her to the five cent store after church and buy her a penny's worth. She hadn't had a chocolate-covered raisin in quite a while, actually they had no candy in the house since Pa got sick. Doci looked up and listened to the news she did not want to hear.

Chapter 59

Joanne Verada was waiting for the call so when the phone rang at her Sewickley home she picked it up after the first ring. On the other end was her attorney. She sat on the leather couch in the family room off the kitchen and spoke with a nervous, but serious tone.

"Yes, I had left the message earlier. Thanks for calling me back."

There was silence in the big house as she listened. Earlier, when Derek lived there with the girls there were dogs and cats and even a pony. There were her daughter's sleep-over friends and there was music and swimming and human little-girl cannon balls in the pool. Now it was all still. Derek was gone. Becky had drowned when she went canoeing all those years ago. Emily had been raped and nearly murdered and the two hadn't talked for ten days over a disagreement about a pregnancy. Both Emily and Joanne could be powerfully stubborn. And neither was giving in. Joanne listened to what her attorney had to say and then responded.

"No, Liz. I don't want you to negotiate a settlement. I want you to contest the will."

She held her ear to the receiver, listened to her reply, and then continued. "I know these things drag on for a long time, and I know everyone gets hurt, and I know the money can be tied up, and I know in the end the attorneys are the only ones that win. You don't have to tell me that."

She listened quietly now pacing in the hallway.

"I don't care if you have to argue that Emily is incompetent. I don't care if you have to argue that Derek was insane when he wrote it up. I just want it nullified. Do you hear me, Liz?"

Joanne Verada was pacing faster. She looked outside. The pool was covered by a tarp and the green grey canvas was covered with patches of snow. There was a low area were water had collected and frozen. A red bird was trying to break the ice to get at the water. Joanne continued.

"I don't want to sleep on it, Liz. I have a mortgage to pay here and other bills, and no source of income. I need you to get me a settlement here, and I don't care who you have to step on to get it done."

There was a long pause. Joanne listened and then spoke forcibly.

"Yes, even if it is Emily."

She put the phone down on the table. Outside the cardinal had made it through the thin ice and having tasted the stagnant water shook his head back and forth quickly. All that work and a bitter result. He quickly took to the ice covered trees at the rear of the property. It wasn't raining or snowing but the clouds were low in the sky and it was moist and cold. It was early afternoon and the light of the day was receding. Joanne walked to the back of the house past the closed door that been Becky's bedroom and into Emily's room. Aside from few of the throw pillows missing from her bed the room was the same as it had always been. Joanne sat on the bed and looked across to the desk. There was a picture tacked to the cork board above. It was of her and Derek, and Emily with Buster the dog. Everybody was smiling that day, she noticed. But what were they smiling about? She could not remember. When she left the room she pushed the lock from the inside and closed the door with a thud.

Chapter 60

Emily sat nervously waiting for her counselor. Her therapist, employed by Mary Herman College and based in the Student Health Center, greeted her with a smile and led her into her office. Emily walked with a limp and sat on the couch. Her therapist's name was also Emily. She was dressed professionally but did not wear a white jacket. She wore Birkenstocks that were newly refurbished. It was Emily's second visit.

After Emily found her place on the couch her counselor finished writing at her desk and came and sat on a chair that faced her.

"And how has your week been going?" She crossed her legs and placed her hands on her thighs quietly. She looked at Emily and smiled softly encouraging her to speak.

Emily began. "I had another attack."

The counselor nodded. "Please tell me what happened?" The counselor clicked her pen and began to take notes. Emily continued.

"I was in history class. It is a big class. Everything was fine. I was taking notes. All of a sudden I had a sensation that I couldn't breath. I thought maybe I was having a heart attack. My vision became blurry and I had a tight feeling in my chest. I had an overwhelming feeling of doom, like bad things were about to happen to me. I had to leave the class. I wanted to run outside to get some air. After a while it passed and I got a migraine headache."

Emily's counselor sighed. "Like things got out of your control?"

"Yes, I guess so. I just want it to stop."

"Emily, how are you sleeping?"

"Not too well. I still get the nightmares. I have been leaving the light on. I really don't like sleeping."

"Emily, did you visit the psychiatrist I asked you to see?"

"No, not yet. I think I have an appointment for next week."

Emily's counselor sat quietly for minutes and then wrote on her yellow pad. Emily sat quietly and waited. Finally, the counselor spoke.

"Emily, have you ever heard of "PSTD", post-traumatic stress disorder?"

"I don't think so. What is that?"

"Well it sometimes happens to people who have been in combat, or like you, have been raped or tortured. Patients have panic attacks, depression, trouble concentrating, things like that."

Emily looked up. "That sounds like me."

"Yes, and you have flashbacks which can be a part of the syndrome."

Emily said nothing. She wondered if she could continue with her classes. Maybe she would need to take some time off. She wondered if she should bring it up with her counselor. She decided that she wouldn't.

"Emily, who is helping you?"

Emily looked slightly confused by the question. She thought about it for a moment then spoke. "No one."

"No one?"

"No one."

"What about your family?"

Emily looked up and smiled. "My older sister drowned in a canoe accident. My father committed suicide when he was wrongly arrested and charged with my kidnapping and murder. And my mother is suing me to contest my inheritance from dad."

The counselor sighed for an extended period. Then she continued. "But you have many friends here on campus?"

"Yes, I do. But my best friend Nicki's dad lost his job and she is not sure she can continue at Mary Herman."

The counselor continued. "Emily, have you ever felt loved, unconditionally loved.?"

Emily again looked confused by the question but answered without pause.

"No. I mean my father loved me, I am certain of that. But I know that there was some problem between my mom and dad regarding me. I don't know what it was. My mother seemed to love me only when I was doing well in school or sports. I have never felt that I was loved no matter what. But I haven't thought about it too much."

There seemed to be a bit of a time lag before Emily started to cry. When the crying began it would not stop.

Emily the counselor handed Emily the patient a tissue and she wiped the salty water off of her face. The counselor looked briefly at the clock and handed her another tissue.

Outside on the green that abutted the Student Health building Emily could hear a student calling her friend. She thought she recognized the voice but she wasn't certain. The days were getting brighter and the wind wasn't quite so cold. Emily told herself it did no good to cry. Somehow things would work out she reasoned. Nevertheless she needed another tissue.

Chapter 61

Bob LeClair entered the waiting room of the Medical Examiner of Allegheny County. The final identification and assembly of the victims was taking place in Pittsburgh because Erie did not have the resources nor the facilities to do this type of work. It was a long, rainy drive to Pittsburgh but he insisted in being involved at every step of the way. In the drab basement office shared by some of the pathology assistants Bob was greeted by Carl. Carl was a large man, short of breath from the slightest of activity and alternately smiling and taking a sigh. Bob liked him.

Carl wiped the sweat that formed on his brow even on a cold day and spoke.

"Hi. Mr. LeClair. I am glad you came today."

Bob greeted Carl. Carl breathed noisily and smiled. He finished. "We have DNA matched Julie's arm and leg."

Bob cleared his throat and asked optimistically, "Is she...Is she complete?"

Carl replied. "No, Bob. We are still missing her right hand."

Bob interrupted. "Is that it?"

"No. We need part of her left foot."

Bob was silent for a few minutes. Carl sat respectfully and caught his breath. The last time Bob had visited Julie did not have her arm or her leg so there is forward motion, he concluded.

"Can I see her?"

Carl looked up and smiled. "Of course you can. Would you like me to stay with you when we go?"

Bob paused for a minute and then answered in a gravely voice. "Yes, Carl. I would like you there the entire time."

Carl smiled and got up very slowly. The two walked down a shiny gray hallway to the forensics area. Inside Bob LeClair stood on one side of the table and Carl stood on the other. In between the two men was the pieced together body of Bob's daughter. Partially covered in a thick pale yellow sheet Julie almost looked "together". Bob touched her gently and cried. After a long time Carl spoke.

"We are getting more tissue and forensics from the New York site this week. I am determined to match Julie's hand and foot. I know you want every bit of your daughter to take home."

Bob looked up and nodded in appreciation for Carl's thoughtfulness. He was still crying.

On the ride back to Ohio the snow let up and the road was dark and wet, but not icy. Below the clouds in the west there was a large orange winter sun. It looked warm. The traffic was light and headlamps were being turned on. There was almost no wind. Bob rode alone in silence as he had done on his Pittsburgh trips before. He saw some snow fall off a big pine tree along the wide medium. Taped to the dash was a picture of Julie smiling at him. He remembered the day that he had taken the photo. She had just come in from a run and she had a glow on her face and she was singing. He couldn't remember the song but he remembered the purity of her voice. Her voice was like a dollop of sugar to him. Alone in his car as the darkness stole the day Bob almost smiled in the memory. But then the tears came back, and they flowed like a hard rain, continuing into the night until he crossed the Ohio line.

Chapter 62

Emily sat at the fixed desk in the large room and wrote her history exam. Even with all of the counseling and the medicine the psychiatrist had prescribed she found herself anxious and unfocused. The essay directed question was straight forward but she found herself referring to it repeatedly. There was a time element to the test and she told herself to focus. She found herself looking outside. It was clearly Spring now and it was an unseasonably warm day. Two blue jays dove from a tree to almost crash into the ground and then miraculously they pulled out of their descent, crossed paths and soared back to limbs above. The branches had green and yellow buds. Emily watched for some time before she reminded herself to focus.

"What was the question?" she whispered out loud. "Oh, yes that's right. I need to get going on this."

Then again her concentration lapsed. She felt that if she was able to take the exam and somehow pass it would be some kind of a moral victory. But she was not the Emily of prior days. No. Then she would have been disappointed with anything less than a "A". She wondered if anyone noticed how restless she was. Where they staring at her, she wondered. She looked outside again. Her anxiety swelled. She knew she needed to concentrate. She told herself to focus. She even counted backwards from ten, breathing like her counselor told her, trying to relax.

Even if she got a poor grade she told herself it might be a passing grade. That would be fine she thought. Just get me out of this room she told herself. Suddenly everything seemed very close in. Her vision went out of focus. She felt her heart pounding. She looked around and wondered if anyone had noticed what was happening to her. She had to remind herself where she was and what she was doing. She was writing an essay for a history exam. Yes, that was it. There was nothing to be afraid of here. Then she felt like she might vomit. Then she knew she had to get out of the room.

Emily stood and felt dizzy. She could see that the proctor had noticed her and was coming her way. She grabbed her backpack and windbreaker and started walking to the door by the far hallway and pushed it open, moving fast now but with a limp. Shortly the proctor came out through another door and queried.

"Is everything alright? Do you want to turn in you exam?"

Emily turned to the proctor feeling particularly frightened, but she tried to answer calmly, as if to smooth out her departure.

"Yes, everything is fine. No, I mean I am sick, very sick. I don't think I can continue with this test. No, I mean everything is fine. Just fine."

The proctor looked confused but walked in Emily's direction. She had a sympathetic, helping, look. Emily walked as fast as she could with her limp as if she were trying to get away. She looked back twice very frightened and the proctor let her go.

Outside she felt the warmth of the early spring day. There was a slight breeze and birds were singing. Students were moving about campus and greeted Emily in a friendly way. Emily smiled back but felt that she needed to get to a safe place. She tried not to show any fear when she smiled to her classmates. She wondered if they knew how disabled she had become.

Chapter 63

Driving in her car Emily started to feel better. The breeze from the partially opened window blew cool on her face. The slight distraction of the stick shift, the hum of the engine, the music on the radio, and the sense of motion were all calming to her. She now knew that taking finals would not be so easy anymore. If they triggered panic attacks she would drop out of school she told herself. Maybe she could take stronger medicine. Yeah, maybe that "shrink" could calm her down with more medicine.   Then she could appear to be a normal student.   Emphasis on the word "appear" she told herself.   She now knew that she would never be "normal" again. Never. Besides she hated taking medicine. It was such a crutch and it just partially masked her symptoms. It didn't solve the problem. It didn't get at the root cause. She was a kidnapping and rape victim she told herself. She had survived torture and an attempted murder. You don't get over that with a pill or two.

Emily pulled her yellow VW into the volunteer space behind the Erie City mission. It was the spot she parked in before her life had changed.   She raised the window and walked to the alley by the train tracks. This was the spot were she and the staff used to bring sandwiches from the mission to the heroin addicts. Today the alley was still. She walked into the dusky shade of an damp brick building and she sat on the cracked pavement.

After a brief moment Emily opened her eyes and looked around. There was a musty smell that was vaguely familiar to her and a needle or two that had been left in a trash pile. She felt calm. For the first time in the day she felt better. She rested on the ground for a long time and became more still. Without the sun it had become cooler. Emily noticed the cold but felt safe in the dark alley.

Suddenly an addict moved into the entrance of the alleyway. Emily could see him in the light of a low sun. He put a band on his arm and pumped the tip of a needle. When he finished he moved quickly back onto the street. Engrossed in his own addiction he neither saw nor acknowledged Emily. She liked being invisible in this way. It brought her a mild comfort.

After some time Emily stood to leave. That's when she felt it for the first time. Initially it was frightening, but when she figured it out she almost smiled. She slid back down the brick wall to a sitting position and placed her hand on her stomach. She was certain of what she felt. For the first time her baby was kicking. Small kicks at first and then he was dancing. She sat in the damp alleyway in the now darkness and marveled at the movement of her unborn child.

Chapter 64

At the meeting the psychiatrist was supposed to be in charge. He arrived late so the social worker passed out the agenda, basically a list of the patients to discuss. The room was a small and belonged to no one, but shared by many, and on this day it was the mental health department of Mary Herman College. The department consisted of a full time counselor, a part time social worker who also served as a secretary and receptionist, and a contract psychiatrist. The tardy doctor was the only one who could bill for administrative time. The others did case reviews on their day off.

When he arrived he apologized. His tone was not convincing. The others acknowledged him and began the cases. The psychiatrist was at the end of his career. His white beard was frayed. His face was red. He had more bills than income. Most of the things he had believed in life had been disproved. He sat in wooden chair and took a copy of the agenda. In an earlier day he would have lit a pipe.

"How many patients do we have?"

The part time social worker-secretary responded. "Eleven students, three faculty, one administrator."

The psychiatrist sighed. "I only have one billable hour.

"Yes. I think it will go fast." The part time social worker reassured. She wore a wool dress and leather shoes. The counselor, who did the bulk of the work for the college wore jeans and suede clogs with an Indian print stitched border. She wore a soft white button down shirt. She smiled and was calm. It was also her day off.

When the group got to Emily the psychiatrist queried. "Where are we with Ms. Verada?"

The counselor replied. "The health plan allows six counseling visits, two psychiatry medication evaluations, and one billed case review."

"And..."

"We have used them all."

The doctor scratched his beard. "Have we made any progress?"

The therapist responded. "Post Traumatic Stress Syndrome is a tough diagnosis. I think Emily has gained a slight bit of insight into her situation."

"I don't care about insight. Has she obtained any symptom relief, less panic attacks, less anxiety, better coping."

Both the counselor and the social worker shook their heads negatively. The social worker answered.

"I know Emily well. If anything her symptoms have become more intense. Her functioning has deteriorated."

The doctor scratched his beard and sighed. The counselor wondered silently if the scratching was causing the bare spots. He continued.

"Have we asked the health plan for a waiver? I mean for continued therapy?"

The secretary answered. "Yes. I have called the plan administrators many times."

"And?"

"Denied."

"Did you appeal?"

"Yes."

"In writing?"

"Yes."

"And?"

"Denied."

"What did they say?"

"They told me that paying for care for sick people would cut into their profits?"

The psychiatrist paused for a moment and then realized that he was being played. Although the knew that the social worker was telling the truth about how the plan operated he also knew that they would not speak truthfully about their motives. The secretary continued in a more professional tone.

"They told me to refer to the plan document. That Ms. Verada had reached her maximum benefit. They told me that there was nothing further that they could do?"

The psychiatrist sighed and waited for a conclusion. The social worker looked at the counselor who gave her the signal to continue. Either would have said the same thing.

"Emily was once an "A" student. She is now failing almost all her subjects. Her father committed suicide and her mother is fighting her over his estate. The monies are apparently tied up in litigation. In her deteriorated condition I doubt she will be returning to Mary Herman next Fall."

The psychiatrist responded. "Not coming back next Fall?"

The others nodded.

"Right. So that makes me feel better. She will be someone else's case then. Right?"

The others nodded. The psychiatrist put a line through Emily's name on his piece of paper. Unfortunately his pen was dry. He shook it and tried again. Seeing this the secretary handed the doctor a her blue Rollerball pen with a smile. He crossed off her name with the slight sense of relief that comes from transferring a difficult problem somewhere else. Then he scratched his beard to the therapist's dismay, looked at the pile of charts, and continued with a question.

"OK, Who is next?"

Chapter 65

In a small conference room in an office in Harrisburg, the seventh regional task force of the FBI met to discuss the open unsolved cases. The region included parts of four states and the "114" cases, as they were designated, were unsolved cluster homicide investigations. In order to get the highest ranking they had to involve victims from more than one state, victims who were police officers or government officials, and cases where homicides were continuing to be committed by the suspects. In Region Seven there were three open and ongoing investigations that met the "114" criteria.

FBI agents Nickles, Jeffreys, and Sloan had been involved in the Emily Verada case from the beginning, and had spent a fair amount of time in Erie. All three agents were based in Washington, D.C. When the Region Seven supervisor moved to the Verada case Sloan spoke clearly.

"Briefly reviewed- A 114 priority case. Nineteen known victims, all female, young college aged. A sheriff's deputy shot and killed. Four victims rescued. Likely suspect Fred Murtins, of Erie. At large now for many months. Last sighting at Muddy River Community Hospital, in Muddy River, PA. A grey Toyota Corolla, registered to his wife, was found in Wilkes-Barre. No new leads."

The FBI supervisor was familiar with all the case documentation. He had relatives in Northwestern Pennsylvania and took this case personally.

"What about forensics?"

Agent Sloan answered. "Everything ties to Murtins. They think there may be more victims. Julie LeClair (deceased) and Emily Verada were marked with the numbers twenty-two and twenty-three, respectively, so likely the victim list will grow."

"What about Mr. Murtin's family?"

Jeffreys answered. "The wife is in custody. I'm not sure on what charge. They believe she is a flight risk, naturally. And the son, aged ten, is in foster care."

"Has the wife or son given us anything to go on?"

"Nothing actionable at this point."

The supervisor continued. "What is your working theory of the case?"

Nickles answered. "Murtins has family ties to the former Soviet Union. Ukraine, I believe. We are concerned that after he sold the Corolla in Wilkes-Barre he took a bus headed north and eventually entered Canada. We don't know if he headed west and crossed the Bering Strait into Russia, or bought a new identity and flew to the Ukraine. Either way we have made contact through the State Department with Ukrainian Officials to watch for him."

"And how likely is that?"

Sloan smiled. "At the current time unlikely. I don't believe we even have an extradition treaty with them currently. But the State Department says if they offer him up they could arrange some sort of a trade."

Nickles continued. "Of course he could still be in the United States. There are 350 million people here and a middle aged man could disappear fairly easily."

The supervisor bore a look of contempt. He would love to get his hands on Murtins. But he realized every day the case got colder.

"No new leads you say?"

"Nothing recent."

"How's the young victim, Verada?"

Sloan answered. "It's been pretty rough, sir. She has dropped out of college I think. Last time I was in Erie she was staying at the shelter. She is on a lot of psychiatric medication and has been struggling. I try to visit her when I am in Erie. She is definitely going through a rough patch."

The supervisor rubbed his face in disgust and spoke. "Well dammit, let's keep this case alive. Can you get one of those crime shows to do another story on our suspect?"

Jeffreys answered. "Yes sir, we can do that again."

The supervisor was ready to move on. He had eight more "114s" to review and later in the day he needed to work on the budget. He had been on the force for twenty-eight years and had always marveled at the brutality of the world that he lived in. There was nothing that would make his day more than closing one of these high profile cases. Unfortunately, he knew all too well what happened once they cooled off. Agent Sloan decided that she would go back to Erie and press Murtin's wife again, harder this time. Also she needed to visit Officer Marta Fuentes's family and the family of the decedent, Julie LeClair. She opened her blue pen with a click and marked her plan in her "to do" folder.

Chapter 66

When Bob LeClair got the call he was shaving. His wife answered the phone and he stuck his head in the hallway, lathered up.

"Yes, Carl. I will tell him." She said on the old phone. There was a pause as she listened. Bob imagined Carl struggling for breath as he talked.

Mrs. LeClair responded. "Yes. I am certain he will want to come to Pittsburgh."

"No, I understand that it is not necessary. But, Bob would prefer it that way."

There was a pause, then Mrs. LeClair thanked the caller, put down phone, and turned to her husband.

"They have found Julie's hand and foot. Their forensic investigation is finished. He said Julie can come home."

Bob LeClair let out a sigh and held back a tear. His wife continued. "That fellow there is very concerned about you, Bob."

"Yes. I know."

"He said you don't need to come to Pittsburgh. He would take care of everything."

"I know. But I have to go. I have to."

"Should I call the funeral home, like we planned?"

Bob looked at his wife. He felt some relief that he would finally have their daughter nearby.   He felt relief that they could finally have a proper service and burial for her.   He nodded in agreement and moved back into the bathroom to finish his shaving. She followed him to the door and watched his reflection in the mirror as he pulled the shaver along his cheek. Then she spoke.

"Bob, this time I would like to go to Pittsburgh with you. I want to be there when we take Julie home."

Bob turned to her and smiled. He hugged her tightly and for a long period. Neither said a word to the other for the rest of the morning.   The only thing that Bob noticed is that the rest of the day seemed slightly lighter to him.

Emily Verada found herself spending more time in the alley near the City Mission.   It was warm enough to sleep outside.   She preferred not to sleep at the shelter.   She managed to get some money from the local addicts who came to the alley to shoot up or deal. Sometimes she did things for them she didn't like and they paid her in cash or drugs, which could relieve her symptoms temporarily.   She rarely felt hungry, but if she needed a meal she could go to the mission or to the McDonald's a few blocks away. Funny, she thought, she had become so unkempt that the other volunteers at the food kitchen didn't recognize her when she came in.   The wound on her hip had reopened slightly and was draining a clear fluid. It wasn't bad she told herself. She had received no prenatal care and her belly was getting quite large.

The sun was orange and large and stayed over the Price Island Bay late into the evening now. The breezes were warm and soft as the dusk approached.   After the people left the downtown area in the evening Emily would sometimes walk out on the sidewalk and look around.   She didn't mind being part of a vacated city in the Fall. She might even lie down on the bench at the nearby bus stop.   Nobody seemed to care what she did after the city was quiet in the early morning hours in the Fall. And that was how Emily liked it.

Chapter 67

Joanne Verada picked up the phone at the Sewickley residence. It was Liz, her attorney on the other end.

"I have good news, Joanne. Emily did not show for her competency hearing."

Joanne was confused. "What does that mean, Liz?"

"Well, as you know we had obtained a court order for her to have a medical and psychiatric evaluation. She did neither. Then at the hearing, which was yesterday, she was a no show."

"And.." was Joanne's reply.

"Well, she may be quickly forfeiting some of her rights."

Joanne queried. "What happens next?"

Liz answered. "I need you to come into town when you can. I think the judge will assign a temporary guardian to assume financial and legal responsibility. Of course we will recommend it will be you."

"How does that work?"

"If we get this ruling the inheritance would be completely managed by you, Joanne."

Joanne paused in thought. Then she continued. "But wouldn't the money still be Emily's?"

"Technically, yes. But as long as you can say the monies dispersed were for the benefit of your daughter I think you would be fine. Of course you need to maintain your residence and household expenses so that she would have a place to come and live, if she wanted to. Besides once we get this ruling I don't think anyone will look too closely where you spend the money."

Joanne felt more upbeat. "Yes. And I do need some cash flow at the present time. And of course you will keep working on the other angles we talked about. But for now this is good. I like the idea of controlling Derek's money."

"Can you come to the office today? I want to file right away."

"Absolutely, Liz. I will be there right after my hair and nail appointment."

"Sounds great. See you soon."

Joanne walked briskly from the kitchen through the laundry room out to the enclosed three car garage. She walked past the BMW X5 in favor of the Porsche Boxster. Yes, she told herself, it was a good day for a convertible. She could put up the top after she had her hair done. It would work out fine she said out loud. It was definitely a good day for a convertible. Then she realized that she had taken the wrong keys from the hooks in the laundry room. She returned through the entrance and grabbed the other set of keys from the hook. They had been Derek's keys originally. He mostly drove the Porsche. On the keychain were house keys, the Porsche keys, and some other keys that Joanne could not identify. Additionally there was a four leaf clover in sterling silver from Tiffany's that Derek had bought when the two went to New York City years earlier. As Joanne pulled the keys free from the hook the silver clover snapped free, hit the washing machine, rolled across the shiny floor and disappeared down a dark storm drain. Joanne paused for a minute, shook her head, and walked out to the Porsche.

Chapter 68

Joanne struggled with the six speed transmission as she made her way down the narrow curved roads from Sewickley Hills. On a couple of occasions she crossed the center line into the curves. She reached for her sun glasses but they slipped from the passenger seat to the floor below. It was difficult to drive the Porsche in heels. Holding a line on the road with one hand she reached across the middle of the car to grab her sunglasses just out of her reach and then with a stretch she got them. That was the exact instant that she hit the garbage truck head on.

Although Joanne was killed instantly the police summoned fire and ambulance and she was cut out of the car and transported to the hospital. The driver of the garbage truck was quite shaken although he appeared unhurt. He was taken to the back seat of the cruiser, asked a few questions, and then transported to the hospital as a precaution. The Porsche was mangled and almost unrecognizable. The neighborhood was sedate and many came from their estates to the sidewalk near the scene to see if they could help or to find out who was hurt. Sewickley Hills is a small private enclave. The word spread fast that Joanne Verada had been in the vehicle.

First to be notified was Joanne's sister in Washington. Next was her attorney Liz.   Her ex husband and oldest daughter had died before her.   And Emily could not be reached. The small room at the hospital were families gather in circumstances such as this was empty. A mechanical clock ticked on the wall. But no one was there to hear it.

At Joanne's attorneys office Liz looked over the papers that her client was about to sign and wondered what to do next. She was sad to lose her friend and golfing partner so tragically. It certainly complicated the case immensely, she told herself.   All of her fees were now tied up in the inheritance. She knew that she had to appear to be sensitive to Emily's needs but she wanted to be paid for her work.

Outside the Sewickley house neighbors had placed flowers at the doorstep. There was a warm summer breeze and a colorful sunset across the hills. The grass was very green and needed to be mowed. It was wet with the evening dew. There was a newspaper in the box below the mailbox. To someone passing by everything looked as it had before. At dusk a few yellow lights clicked on inside and gave the home a pleasant look from the curb. It appeared as if it was the house of a happy and successful family.

Chapter 69

It was twelve days before Emily got the news. A police officer and a case worker stood at the end of the dark alley. The officer lit his bright light and beamed it in Emily's direction. The officer and the case worker had been at the edge of the alley at least five times over the prior days. Emily had been with a man in Cleveland. He had given her money and prescription drugs and she had done things for him she didn't want to discuss. Now she was back in the alley. She sat among the needles, garbage, and filth. She looked pregnant.

The shadows spoke in a conciliatory tone. "Emily Verada, is that you?"

Emily waited before she replied. She had illegal drugs in her pocket. Maybe she was in trouble for that. The things she was doing for those boys was illegal. Even though she was happy with her pregnancy she had been having some bleeding lately. She felt shame. She wondered why she should be in trouble. She only wanted to be alone. She only wanted a moment free from anxiety. The shadows moved closer. Emily responded.

"Yes, that's me."

"Can we speak with you?" The case worker asked.

"OK. What did I do wrong?"

Emily felt anxious. She hoped she wouldn't have a panic attack. Then she might have to run. If she ran they might think she had something to hide. The case worker reached down to touch Emily but could only get so close because of the aroma. Emily moved away slightly.

The officer moved the light slightly away from Emily's face. The case worker continued.

"Your mom was in a terrible accident."

Emily interrupted quickly. "Was she killed?"

The case worker paused for long time and the officer looked away. A large tear formed in Emily's eye and ran down her face. She looked cold in the alley.

"Yes, Emily. She was taken to the hospital but she didn't make it."

Emily put her hands over her face and looked down. She remembered when she was in middle school and loved to run on the trails out behind the Sewickley house. In the late spring the trails were soft and the sun danced between the budding trees. She ran fast and never felt fear. In those days she ran in the forest for hours. She didn't remember being tired. One day she took a break and walked a narrow path toward a bubbling brook. In a small tree she found a robin's nest. Inside there were three blue eggs. On subsequent days she visited the nest and marveled at the eggs. The mother robin stayed nearby and flapped her wings so Emily didn't get too close. One day after a rainstorm Emily stopped to visit the robin's nest. She was sad to see that the little blue eggs were gone. She looked around for the mother robin but she was gone as well. After that Emily never felt the same running in the forest.

She stood slowly and faced the officer and the case worker directly. She had a face that was sad and confused but she spoke clearly.

"OK. So I am not in any trouble?"

The officer responded. "No. Emily, you are fine."

Emily was crying now. The case worker tried to console her. "Emily, I am sorry about your mom's passing."

Emily looked up revealing her wet face and spoke. "Thank you. Thank you both for coming."

Rhetorically the case worker told Emily that she would come back to check on her. It felt hollow. Emily watched the two shadows walk out of the alley quickly. There was a hint of light on the street outside the entrance of the alley and Emily watched the two turn and disappear. Then she could see the patrol car speed away. It was a cold night for early fall. In the sky there were many stars. There was a wisp of a moon behind the clouds. Emily wondered who would have stolen those robin's eggs.

Chapter 70

The activities for the Fall semester were in full swing on the campus of Mary Herman College. Over the summer the cleaning and painting crews worked tirelessly to spruce up the dorms and it showed. The common areas smelled of cut grass and flowers. Tanned students walked in many directions toting backpacks with new laptops. There was an energy in the air. Notably absent from the senior class were Nicki and Emily. Nicki's father became part of the long term unemployed and there were no funds for her to return. She took a job at the local hardware store as a cashier and hoped to save enough for next year.

Emily's absence was even more conspicuous. A few of the yellow ribbons that circled the large oak trees remained. There were whispers about her status. Some said that she had become a drug addict and a prostitute. Others had become convinced that she had committed suicide and the college officials were covering it up. Nobody would park in the space where she did for fear that they too would be cursed and the junior student who got her room in the lottery refused to move in. Without any credible individual to counter the rumors they simple took on a life of their own. No one wanted Emily's fate.

At the LeClair house things remained quietly sad. Bob had believed that if he got Julie home and gave her a decent burial his spirits would improve. Unfortunately the hole in his heart simply scarred over and remained open, heavy, and painful. He made his daily visit to Julie's grave site. He said a prayer. He sat at the dinner table with his wife but after grace it was almost always silent. If this was the healing process Bob told himself it wasn't taking him anywhere. In many ways he preferred when he felt angry. At least that was a less passive emotion. At least his anger might take him places.

In the early hours of the morning when Bob couldn't sleep he sat at his computer and studied the reports that his contacts at the FBI emailed from Washington, DC. By now the case had officially become cold. The reports led to Austin, Texas and New Haven, Connecticut. They led to the Ukraine and to the Black Sea. He wondered if a capture of his daughter's killer would bring him any peace. After all nothing would bring Julie back. Sometimes he surfed to the Princeton University web page and imaged if Julie were there. She certainly had the academics and the character they were looking for. He looked at the page that featured the Women's Varsity Tennis Team. He studied the bright, happy faces of the student athletes. That's when the tears came again. He studied the matches and the scores and knew that Julie would have done well in that league. Yes, she was a competitor he told himself. After a while Bob returned to bed and watched the flicker of moonlight on the ceiling until it became the first light of dawn. Only then did he briefly rest.

Chapter 71

The days became shorter and the nights colder. The leaves changed into brilliant colors and the sky became star bright at nighttime. Emily struggled with the cold in the evenings but tried to stay out of the shelter. She felt the least anxiety in the alley. She had less flashbacks and panic attacks if she stayed away from other people. She knew that she couldn't live in the alley forever. She wasn't in a planning mode, however. Rather she tried to avoid or diminish the next crisis. Survival was her only goal. A short spell without a panic attack or a flashback was her only hope. Everything else was secondary. She had taken a blanket from the shelter. She wrapped it around her tightly. Her baby kicked inside. She found it difficult to find a comfortable position.

A cold wind alternated from the north and the west. Emily struggled to stay warm. She knew she could go to the shelter if necessary. They would take her until 10 p.m.. After that she was on her own. She had sixty-four dollars in her pocket. It was the money that one of the addicts had paid her. Shit, she told herself, she could stay in a hotel if she wanted. She wondered if she should walk to the McDonald's and get a diet coke. They didn't want her sitting inside. She was too filthy and she smelled. At least that's what they told her. She would offend the other customers. But they would let her buy it "to go". They never bothered her when she bought food "to go".

At that moment Emily noticed a shadow at the end of the alley. She studied it in the distance. It was in the shape of a very small person, maybe a child. As the shape came closer Emily realized it was not a child, but rather an elderly woman. A small, kyphotic, woman walked closer with the assistance of a crutch of some sort. No, Emily told herself, it was a cane. When the woman got very near she spoke.

"Emily? Emily Verada?"

"Yes. That's me. What do you want?"

The elderly woman smiled briefly and spoke. "I'm Doris. Everyone calls me Doci." She caught her breath and continued. "I had a difficult time finding where you were staying. I am glad to know you."

She reached out her hand. Emily studied her carefully in the moonlight. She didn't know any frail elderly woman. This person was too nicely dressed to be homeless. Her nature was too calm and friendly to be some kind of social service or church worker. Beside they never bothered her in the evening. They were home with their families. What could she possibly want? Emily took her hand and started to stand. Doci stopped her.

"No need to get up."

"What do you want?"

"I just wanted to come down and meet you. My granddaughter helped to rescue you."

Emily paused and looked at the eyes of the woman. She was not threatening at all. Emily felt no fear. It seemed strange to her.

"Well, maybe she should have left me there to die. Maybe we would have all been better off then."

Doci replied with a smile. "No. No. No. Marta was not like that. Things are tough now, but they can get better. I know they can."

Emily smiled. She felt the elderly woman was speaking nonsense.

"How did you get here? How did you find me?"

"I asked around. I took buses. I glad I can meet you finally."

"Shouldn't you be back at the nursing home?"

Doci smiled. "Probably so. I did have a slight stroke, you know. That's why I have the cane. If I improve I am hoping to get rid of it, actually."

Emily thought for a long time. The pause seemed fine. Then she spoke. "I had a cane also. I was able to give it up."

Doci sighed. Then she handed Emily a brown bag and spoke. "I made you a ham sandwich and some other things. I imagined that you might be hungry out here by yourself. I baked the bread myself, and the tomatoes and lettuce are from my small garden. I made some potato salad the way that Marta liked it and baked some chocolate chip cookies for you."

Emily looked at Doci incredulously. Doci continued. "And I put two cans of Diet Coke in there to wash it down. Marta liked when I left them in fridge near the freezer so they are especially cold. I hope that is OK?"

Emily wondered what the catch would be. She queried. "What do you want from me?"

Doci looked at her for a long time. She wasn't smiling but her face was cheerful. She didn't seem to be bothered by the cold. She sighed and responded to Emily.

"There isn't anything, dear. The things I most want you can't give me. Marta isn't coming back and Pa is gone. I can no longer sing or dance, and my youth is only a distant memory."

She smiled with a wisdom that Emily had rarely seen. She couldn't remember someone giving her something without wanting something in return. It just didn't happen that way. Emily felt oddly calm. Doci nodded and started to walk out of the alley. She was small and slow and she guided herself with her cane. When she got halfway out and into the darkness she turned to Emily and spoke.

"If it is OK with you dear I would like to come back and visit with you again. Would that be alright?"

Emily squinted to see the small woman in the near distance. She studied her again and looked at the brown bag and her bounty. She probed her internal barometer. It was calm. She spoke. "Yes, certainly. I would like that. Thanks for the meal. Tell me again, what is your name?"

The elderly woman spoke softly. "I'm Doris. But please call me Doci."

Emily nodded and Doci walked slowly out onto the street in the distance. Emily watched her until she was gone and then she studied the night sky above. There were too many stars to count and some appeared to be twinkling. Emily pulled out one of the chocolate chip cookies that Doci had left. They were fat and large and full of chunks of chocolate. Emily decided she would eat the cookies first.

Chapter 72

Doci stood by the dresser in the home where she had lived for sixty-two years. She was alone. Her knuckles and her wrists were painful and swollen. It was nothing new. A cold wet snowstorm had come to the region and left rain, ice, and snow. That's when her arthritis was at it's worst. She had made a tuna salad sandwich for Emily. She had some potato salad and Rice Krispy squares for her. There were two Diet Cokes in the fridge. She had visited the alley were Emily was living many times in the last weeks. Sometimes she was there. Sometimes she was not. Doci told herself that this was how a girl in trouble behaved. She had to keep trying.

For a moment she hesitated. She had been up for hours. There were three buses to navigate. The wind was cold and the sidewalks could be slippery. She knew that she was frail. If she fell she would certainly break a bone. Then who could she help? She was eighty-three, she reminded herself. She looked in the mirror and saw her reflection. Her hesitation melted away. She would bring extra mittens and a scarf. After all she had the downtown bus to catch.

Doci walked slowly up the sidewalk to the alley. The wind was strong and there were many slippery spots. She held her cane with one hand and Emily's dinner with the other. Turning at the alley she proceeded down the dark corridor. Nothing. Emily was not there. She looked at the spot where her young friend slept to see if there were any clues. Nothing. She walked out carefully and sat at the bench nearby. It was partially blocked by a clear plastic wind screen that was covered with a lipstick advertisement. Doci was happy to have some protection from the wind. She waited.

After some time a tall, skinny, man entered the alley. Doci followed him deep into the shadows. When he turned and saw her he looked quite frightened. He spoke in a staccato.

"What do you want, lady?"

"I'm looking for Emily? Have you seen her?"

"What's it to you?"

"She's a friend of mine. That's all. I brought her some dinner."

The thin man looked up more interested. He knew Emily well. The homeless were quite aware of the whereabouts of their colleagues but they needed to be careful who they gave information for fear of retaliation.

"You mean young, pregnant Emily?"

"That's the girl." Doci was having trouble with her balance. She planted her cane and took a better grip. If there were a place to sit down she would. She told herself that she would be OK.

The thin man studied Doci. There were dark circles around his eyes. The skin hung over his gaunt face. He had trouble maintaining much eye contact. He wanted Emily's dinner. He spoke. "She got bad contractions and bleeding and they called an ambulance. I think she was due to give birth anyway. I guess todays the day." He looked away and smiled.

Doci queried. "Do you know which hospital they took her to?"

"Saint Veronica's, I think."

"Thank you, Sir."

The thin man smirked in the dark light. Doci wondered how someone's little boy had become this unfortunate soul. She spoke quietly.

"Would you like some dinner, son. I have some tuna salad and some other things. It might be a good snack for you. And if Emily is at Saint Veronica's she won't be needing anything."

The thin man nodded pleasantly. Doci handed him the bag. When she did she brushed her hand against his. He pulled away strangely but looked up and signaled appreciation. There was no wind in the alley. As she walked out to the sidewalk she could hear him tearing open the bag. It will be good for him to eat something she told herself.

Outside there was no bus to Saint Veronica's Hospital. It was about twelve blocks away. Doci told herself to walk slowly. She told herself not to mind the wind and the ice. She hummed a song from church and told herself it was good to stop and rest, if necessary. She did not stop. She kept moving along the icy sidewalk.

Chapter 73

When Doci arrived at Saint Veronica's she made her way to the small snack shop on the first floor and ordered a hot tea.   She took the styrofoam cup to the lobby and slowly drank and unbundled until she was warm again.   She noticed that they already had their holiday decorations up.   Some ice that had frozen in her hair was melting and a cold stream of water ran down her back.   She shivered with a smile.   Nobody noticed.   Many busy people walked by.   It seemed that everybody was in a hurry.   Doci tried to smile at some of the people but she was mostly ignored.

She drank her tea which helped her regain her strength and balance.   Then she walked to the information desk and queried the volunteer in the red coat.

"Verada, Emily Verada?"

The volunteer had beautiful white hair neatly combed. She looked at the computer screen and spoke.

"Room four fifty-four.   Take the second elevator to the fourth floor and walk to the end of the hall.   That is the maternity entrance. You will need to sign in there."

She smiled. Doci returned the smile. At the Maternity entrance Doci signed the book and was escorted to Emily's room. Inside Emily looked pale. Her eyes were closed and then opened slowly. She had been sleeping. Doci reached out a hand and Emily grabbed it.

"How did you find me here?"

Doci smiled. "Maybe I should be a detective."

Emily retorted. "Only you are too old and too small."

"Yes. You are right."

The room was quiet for what seemed a long time. Then Doci spoke again. "Did everything go well with the delivery?"

"Yes, of course."

"Are you in pain?"

"No. I'm fine. Actually, they said I could leave later today?"

"And your baby, boy or girl?"

"Boy."

"And.."

"He is fine."

The room was silent until Emily let a tear that she was fighting escape. Then it was clear that she couldn't fight how upset she was. Doci just listened. Emily explained.

"The social workers and the government came in and took my newborn. They said I was not fit. They called me a drug addict and a prostitute. They had papers. There was nothing I could do."

Doci sat at the side of Emily's bed and held her hand. She said nothing. After a long time she suggested again that Emily come and live with her. She went through all the reasons it made sense. Emily said nothing. Doci had tried to convince Emily before many times. Now she had a new reason to get well she told her. Emily was the most lost, upset, and angry that Doci had ever seen.

After a long visit Doci stood and put on her coat, hat, and scarf. She reflexively bent over to kiss Emily the way you would kiss someone in your own family. She turned and walked slowly across the room to the door when Emily started to speak.

"Doci." she said.

"Yes." was her reply.

"Hold on, please. I am coming with you."

Doci looked startled. Emily continued.

"Is that alright?"

Doci smiled. "Yes, of course. That would be wonderful."

Emily got up slowly from the hospital bed and walked to the closet to get dressed. At that moment the nurse came in and helped her get her things. Outside the two braved the wind and the cold and walked in the direction of the bus stop. Doci was tired but she was thinking about what to make for dinner.

Chapter 74

The love that Doci provided was the vitamin that Emily's soul lacked. She cheerfully fed and praised her. She listened when Emily opened up. She read to her at bedtime and she sat with her when the attacks came. When Emily left for the alley Doci said nothing. And when she showed up in the night and cried Doci held her. Emily gave up on the whoring and cut back on the drugs. She seemed to need them less and less.

Sometimes when Emily went missing Doci would run hot water in the bathtub and mix in some salts. Then she would bake some bread and wait for her. If she came in late Doci would tell her that she loved her and that she missed her and that she was so happy to see her. And she was.

After all, Emily filled an empty space in Doci's life. She was a friend in need. She was easy to love, Doci thought. And Doci had lots of love to give. Since Emily had come into her life her cane had gone away. She had an interest in cooking again, and she started to volunteer again at the church. On one night very late Emily came in high on drugs and distraught, and after Doci made her some tea Emily told her that she loved her and that she was not going back to the alley. Doci told her that she might not live much longer, but she hoped Emily would stay with her as long as she could. They both smiled and hugged cheerfully. After that Doci was determined to stay alive so she could take care of Emily and Emily was determined to stay away from the temptations that came in the alley.

Doci's actions were not all altruistic, however. She had a secret that predated her relationship with Pa. It had been suppressed for over 65 years now and she felt it bubbling to the surface. She couldn't bring herself to think about it, much less discuss it with Emily. But caring for her young friend she felt a combination of relief and anxiety. Emily sensed they were bonded by something greater than she knew, but she didn't want to rock the boat. She was simply happy to feel unconditional love for the first time that she could remember.

On a warm spring day the two rode in Emily's beetle back to the campus of Mary Herman College and they walked slowly across the green. Doci was so proud of Emily and loved seeing the place. Emily gave her the tour fit for a Queen and they had a snack in the cafeteria. Emily was so busy making sure that her surrogate grandmother didn't get too tired that she forgot about the panic attacks. Doci said she wished she had a chance to go to college when she was young but she said it wasn't commonly done in those days. Afterwards they stopped for a pizza on the way home and Doci ordered a beer.

Chapter 75

The priest at the local church asked Doci to volunteer to help at a second support group. Her first group met on tuesday evenings. The participants were single moms who were struggling with all the issues that resulted from separation, divorce, and raising children, often on their own. Doci made certain that there was coffee and a small snack available. She assisted the group leader in setting up the room in the church basement. She helped new members sign in and find their way from the parking lot to the church basement. She offered a kind word or two. If the group leader had a pamphlet or a book to pass out Doci would help. If a participant needed a tissue or somebody to walk them to their car Doci was there. The participants appreciated her help, the leader appreciated her help, the priest appreciated her help, and the church appreciated her help. But with appreciation comes further need. Doci couldn't say no so she agreed to come on thursday evenings to help with a second group. When Emily came home Doci explained.

"Dear, I have to work at the church on thursday. Can I make your dinner and leave it in the fridge?"

Emily looked at her and answered. "That would be fine, Doci. Can I be of any help?"

"Well I don't know what they need, dear. It is my first time on thursday nights. I don't even know who is meeting."

"I could drive us over there, Doci. And I could wait for you outside."

"That would be wonderful, Emily. Of course you could come inside where it is warm."

"Yes, I could do that. I would be happy to help."

Doci praised. "That would be very nice. I am glad you want to help. We will leave thursday at about 6:30 p.m.. I think we would be home around 9 p.m.."

"We could eat dinner when we get home."

"Yes, Emily, that sounds just fine."

Emily left later in the day and was not around for over two days. Doci missed her and hoped that everything was alright. She knew that Emily was and adult and needed her freedom respected. But she was also aware that she was recovering from a terrible trauma and that process was certain to have setbacks. She promised that if Emily returned and was well she would ask no questions. That was the promise that she made to herself and she intended to stick to it.

When her tea turned cold Doci walked through her empty house and up to her bedroom. She got into her night clothes and got into bed but she couldn't rest. After many hours she heard the key in the door and Emily quietly coming inside. She sighed deeply and started to feel sleepy for the first time in days. She whispered a small prayer of thanks in which she expressed hope that whatever Emily had to do was helping her to get well. Then she fell asleep.

Chapter 76

The group met in the basement of the church. Emily didn't like basements. It was a cold and icy night with nary a cloud in the sky. The two were early and parked the car near the side entrance. Doci made a few trips to get the keys to the basement and turn on the lights. There was coffee to brew and Doci had made brownies which Emily laid out on a table with yellow checked pattern table cloth. Emily moved about tentatively. When the group leader came he introduced himself.

"Hey. My name is Skip."

Skip was tall and cheerful, with long thinning hair. He reached out and held first Doci's hand and then Emily's. Emily wondered if she recognized him from the alley. She said nothing.

Doci answered. "I'm Doci, and this is my granddaughter, Emily." Emily felt honored. She was surprised that Doci would think of her as her granddaughter. Maybe she does love me after all, she told herself.

Doci continued. "We are both from the church. We are here to help you with anything you need. We have some coffee and some brownies, and I can help you arrange the chairs. Do you need to use the restroom?"

Skip replied. "Thanks, no."

Doci comforted. "Do you have a sign in sheet?"

Skip smiled in appreciation for the prompt. "Yes, I have one here somewhere." He fiddled in his pocket and produced a folded sheet. At the top it had the title PSTD Group.

Doci continued. "And how many do you expect?"

Skip replied. "I don't know. Ten or twelve, I guess."

Doci nodded kindly.

For the next fifteen minutes Doci manned the entrance to the room and Skip paced nervously. Emily stayed by the coffee pot and waited. She refilled Skip's styrofoam cup and fed him a brownie. No one came. Doci looked through the small window to see if any cars were entering the church lot. There were none.

After what seemed like a long time Doci spoke. "Sometimes this church is hard to find, and people get nervous about coming to meetings in new places."

Skip appreciated the help. He smiled. Emily refilled his coffee. No one knew what to do.

Doci continued conversationally. "What type of people come to this group usually?"

Skip felt relieved with the ease of her question. "PSTD can affect all kinds of people, from combat veterans to rape victims. It's people who have suffered a major trauma in their life that they couldn't control, such as abuse."

Doci paused for a minute and took in his explanation. She seemed ready to share some information, but before she could he broke the silence.

"That was me. I was abused as a child. By my uncle."

Doci looked at him. He continued.

"Of course that led to other problems. I've had a lot of psychiatric issues and I have been involved with street drugs."

Doci went to get Skip another brownie.   Emily was standing by the coffee and missed the conversation.   Skip took the brownie and while chewing he stopped talking. For the entire time he ate Doci thought about sharing something about her own childhood.   But maybe it was just too deep. Maybe it shouldn't come out now. Finally she felt a need to break the silence.

"Sometimes it takes a while to get these groups going. I hope you will come back next thursday."

Skip smiled sheepishly.   "You don't think we should quit?"

Doci smiled for a long time. She reached out and held Skip's forearm. "No, I think we should keep trying."
After a short while Doci slipped off the lights in the church basement and the three walked out into the cold together. The heat in Emily's car came on quickly and when Doci felt it warming her legs she turned to Emily.

"Thanks, dear. Thanks for helping me."

Doci could see Emily's smile for nearly the entire drive home.

Chapter 77

Emily had been gone for over two days. Doci wondered about her but was certain not to bring it up. An official looking letter had arrived in Emily's name. Doci wondered what it could be. She prepared a nice dinner for Emily but after some time it was cold and Doci put it in the fridge. Later in the evening when she lay in bed she wondered if Emily would recover. She wondered if Emily would be well again. After all you just don't get over something like she went through. You just can't forget about it. Doci knew about getting over things. It just didn't happen easily. Maybe it never happens she thought. But she could be good to her. Emily needed that Doci thought. Nobody was good to her when she needed help. But that didn't matter. That was in the past now. She could be good to Emily.

When Emily finally returned she saw the letter on the table and opened it. It was from her mother's attorney and looked official. She noticed the the letterhead and the quality of the paper.   She read that since the tragic and untimely death of their client, Emily's mom, they would no longer be contesting the will of Derek Verada. They would no longer be trying to prove Emily incompetent and unworthy. They were letting her have the money her father intended. Of course, they would need large legal fees paid, but they expected to extract those from Joanne's estate. They further indicated that Emily would additionally be the heir to her mother's estate minus legal fees and court costs. In addition to Derek's gift of almost fifteen million dollars Emily would likely inherit millions more once Joanne's estate was settled. Finally, they recommended a meeting and offered their legal and financial planning services to Emily.

Emily smiled. "Now they want me as a client."

Doci was at the bottom of the stairs. She greeted Emily and moved into the kitchen where she could warm up something to eat. She noticed Emily with the letter.

"Dear, I've made some dinner if your hungry."

Emily smiled and sat at the kitchen table where Marta used to sit.

Doci continued. "Did you get anything important?"

"They are letting me know they settled my dad's will and they will be sending me some money."

Doci looked concerned. She served a plate of warmed chicken and rice. She poured some Sprite. She waited for a long time before she asked and then she spoke quietly.

"Your not going to be leaving me, are you? I mean you are not moving out?"

Emily looked at her reassuringly. "No Doci, I want to stay here with you."

Doci smiled and poured warm gravy over the rice. Wherever Emily had gone and whatever she had inherited she was happy to have her in her home. Doci suddenly felt hungry again and prepared herself a plate of dinner and sat with Emily.

The food tasted good. Doci hadn't realized how hungry she was.

Chapter 78

It wasn't until the third thursday evening that Skip, Doci, and Emily had a guest. A quiet, sandy haired male filled out the sign in sheet in careful print. He made minimal eye contact and moved nervously. Doci noticed the scars on his wrists and that he walked with crutches. He had a stub of a right leg ending above his knee. She served him coffee in a styrofoam cup. She smiled reassuringly. He took off his jacket and hung it over a distant chair. He was wearing a Yale Baseball tee shirt. It was faded and hinted of a dream not realized. Skip tried to act nonchalant. He wondered if he could run a group with only one attendee.

He pushed forward and introduced himself.

"I'm Skip. I'm the group leader."

The one legged baseball player stood up. He was taller than Skip and very well proportioned. His muscular softness belied his actual size and he hunched over his crutches. He spoke in a near whisper.

"Barnaby. A lot of people call me Snow."

"Snow?"

"Yes, sir. Snow."

"All right then, Snow."

Emily brought Snow a brownie on a white napkin. She was immediately attracted to him. It wasn't only his fabulous looks, rather his vulnerability. He was a deeply troubled individual with a tremendous potential. She recognized that immediately. He nodded in appreciation and said nothing.

For a long time the room was silent. There was a fan in the distance that cycled on and off and if a bus passed outside there was the noise that came from running through the puddles of melted ice. Otherwise nothing. Skip seemed to be waiting for other people to arrive. When no one came he turned his attention to Snow.

Snow was difficult to engage. He hadn't come on his own account. He was trying to satisfy a friend who begged him to join a PSTD group. He was shy before his troubles began. Now he shunned people. He didn't want to talk about the small city in Iraq where three months earlier he had lost his leg in an explosion. He didn't want to talk about the one soldier that he rescued from the ensuing gunfire and carried back to the rear of the convoy before he collapsed from the bleeding in his leg. He didn't want to talk about the medals and the honors. He didn't want to talk about the night terrors and the flashbacks. He didn't want to talk about the panic attacks, or the doctors, and medications that failed to give help other than for a brief time. He only wanted to feel better. He hoped that maybe someone else would say something and then things would feel different. He sensed that this group would cause him nothing but further anxiety and he wanted to leave. But he was the only one there. It would be too obvious if he ran out.

In an odd way Emily sensed what Snow was feeling. She already seemed to know that if Snow felt safe he might say that the thing that troubled him most was not that he was sick or that he lost his leg. It wasn't the doctors, or the paperwork, or the denial of benefits. Rather, without hearing his story, she already knew that it was the fact that he couldn't save the others that was ripping him apart. That day on a routine run to a supply depot eight miles southwest of Bagdad when the improvised explosive device ripped through their vehicle Snow survived and was not able to help the six that didn't. Emily seemed to know this telepathically, because although she never made the leap of logic in her own case, the same thing was at the core of Emily's recovery. She would have to learn to deal with the fact that she wasn't able to save the other girls who Murtins held captive, tortured, and killed.

Skip had begun his questioning. "So Snow why did you decide to join us tonight?"

"A friend sent me." he whispered.

"A friend."

Snow nodded. "A friend who is also a counselor."

"And what does this friend think is wrong with you?"

Snow was silent. He was stammering slightly. He was becoming more anxious. Emily sensed his anxiety. The two briefly met eyes and Snow spoke, if only not to let her down.

"I have physical and emotional problems."

If Skip had let him finish Snow might have said more, but the interruption was welcome for it briefly took the spotlight off the war hero.

Skip's intentions were good but people need to feel comfortable and safe before they can talk. Skip was all business. "Can you share with us what your emotional problems are?"

There was a long pause. Doci stayed by the coffee pot and fiddled with something. Emily sensed Snow's anxiety. She hoped Skip would not beat him up too much. Maybe he would never return. She wanted to hear the rest of Snow's story. What was it like in Iraq on those days? What disappointments had he faced earlier. Maybe she could help him, she thought. That was an odd feeling Emily told herself. She hadn't thought about helping anyone in a long time. She was overwhelmed simply struggling to help herself.

Snow answered in a whisper. "Drugs, alcohol, anxiety, bad dreams, flashbacks. The usual stuff."

"Nightmares?"

"Yes."

"Inability to focus."

"Yes."

"Fear in public places?"

"Yes."

At each question Snow waited longer to answer. Surprising even herself Emily moved forward and sat at a chair that was nearly equally from Snow and Skip and began to talk. Doci, surprised, stepped forward to listen.

"I'm not too good at talking and I haven't said much to anybody about this but I have been suffering terribly in the last year."

Skip turned his attention to Emily. She was looking down and couldn't see how Snow reacted but Doci noticed the sigh of relief, as if the spotlight had moved. Emily began to talk and tell her story. She stopped to cry and then she shared some more. She told all the details and cried sometimes for long periods. The others only listened and did not interrupt. Doci tried to hide her tears at first but eventually cried aloud. When Emily was finished it was very quiet and the room was not the same. Snow came over and put his arm on her shoulder and tried to comfort her. When the crying was over the four walked outside into the night.

Chapter 79

Up until two days prior Snow and Emily had been inseparable. Emily made a suggestion that upset Snow and he gave her some advice and a fight erupted and Emily had a panic attack. Now she was gone and Snow wanted to apologize. He sat at the table and Doci poured him some soup.

Snow queried Doci. "Do you think she will be back this evening?"

"I think so, dear." was the reply. Doci continued. "She leaves like this sometimes. I think she needs to clear her head."

"I shouldn't have gotten upset when she suggested I consider a leg prosthesis. I have been resisting it."

Doci said nothing. She was warming some muffins in the oven. Snow continued, as if in a conversation. Doci was only listening, waiting for the right time to speak.

"I shouldn't have told her that we need to find Murtins and kill him. That upset her I think."

Doci said nothing.

"Do you think I need a leg prosthesis?"

Doci was quiet for a long time. She put the muffins out on a plate for Snow. He had completely finished the soup.

Only the bottom of the bowl was slightly discolored. At the center of the muffin it was quite warm and fragrant. There was a slight mist when Snow split it open with his finger.

"Snow, I will love you no matter what you decide."

He smiled appreciatively. Doci continued. "How are the muffins?"

"Perfect. I love them. Thanks."

"I have more. Do you want more?"

"Maybe one more, thanks."

Doci put another muffin in the oven to be warmed.

"Where do you think she went?" Snow asked.

Doci shook her head. "I never ask."

Snow shared. "She talks about making trips to the home where they are keeping her baby. She doesn't get too close but she walks in the neighborhood or sits in her car."

Doci served the last muffin. Snow continued.

"I know she wants her baby back. That I know for sure."

Snow ate the last muffin. Doci looked at him for a long time and then spoke.

"Maybe you are right. Maybe we should track down that man and get our revenge."

Snow was surprised by the force with which Doci spoke. She was elderly. She was frail. He had never heard her utter a unkind word. But he had taken her Marta. And he irreversibly altered the lives of people she had loved. Pa was gone and Emily was struggling to get her footing. But, revenge? Snow wondered if that was in Doci. He studied her for a long time and wondered what else was inside her head.

Doci had been in bed for hours when Emily returned. She could hear some whispering and some movement about the house. She thought she might have even heard some crying. After a while it was still and it felt warm again. Outside the moon was high and there were only wisps of a breeze in the treetops. It had become cold again.

Chapter 80

When the flashbacks came they were sudden and severe. Snow had noticed less of them since he met Emily but they would not go away. They would never go away, he concluded. In the early morning hours on the day that he and Emily planned to travel to Harrisburg to visit her roommate Nicki Snow drifted in and out of wakefulness. Then, like the worst night terror imaginable, he found himself driving on that dusty road outside of Bagdad. He was using reasonable care. He knew and accepted the risks. But it was his second trip of the day and the scorching heat had drained him. Without warning there was a flash, then flames, then screams, and then he heard the explosion. He gave return gunfire, but it didn't feel focused. Nothing felt focused. As his mind flashed through the events as if he were watching it live but at a distance he felt his chest pound and his mouth go completely dry. His eyes could not find clarity. He had been hit in the leg with something hot and now it felt numb. He managed to drag himself to the side of the road away from the explosion and he lay there clammy and gasping for air. For a time he was certain of death. He tasted it. That copper flavor was in his mouth, like the last time he was wounded. His breathing produced no strength. And then it moved away. He could see a number of his fellow soldiers still in the road lifeless and burned, some yelling for help. He was able to move to one and help him to the wall. When he moved back to the others there was gunfire and a second explosion. Flames spread across the road and lit up the sky. He smelled the flesh. He moved back in the direction of the wall. He was reliving all the feelings now. A broken record played over and over as if it were trying to rid his mind of it. But it became more concentrated, the venom in his brain as potent as ever. It would not leave. It would never leave he told himself.

His skin was wet. The sheets were wet and the blanket was in a crinkled ball. A small clock had been knocked off the bedside table and lay on the floor still ticking. Snow was completely awake now sitting in the bed. His breathing was deeper and more productive. His heart continued to pound.

Outside the room and down the stairs Doci and Emily prepared breakfast and food for the trip. Snow could hear them talking. He could smell the coffee percolating. He wondered when the next flashback would come. He wondered if he could continue to survive them. He hoped there would be a breakthrough in medical research so he could be given medicine. He wondered why he hadn't burned up that day like the others. His job was simple. He needed to go downstairs and pretend everything was fine.

Doci handed the last bag of supplies to Emily and gave her a big hug. Snow bent down and kissed Doci on the cheek and then hugged her. Doci thought it was wonderful that Emily would use some of her inheritance moneys to help Nicki return to Mary Herman College next fall. What she didn't know is that she planned to give Nicki's family some money to help them through the rough patch.

The yellow beetle had been warming up in the driveway when the two hopped inside. Doci held the porch railing with one hand and waved with the other. She thought to herself how wonderful Snow looked with his new leg. No one would even know she thought. She blew them both a kiss and went inside. From the window she saw the car move down the street and over the hill and disappear in the distance. A bright winter sun was rising over the snow covered fields in the distance. But the weather forecast predicted a change by afternoon.

Chapter 81

Doci's illness started with a small cough. It was minor enough and she tried to ignore it.   Snow and Emily were concerned. When the fevers came and she felt weak she said nothing.   The doctor at the urgent care was reassuring and gave her an antibiotic. She felt uplifted for a few days but the cough returned with wheezing and when she went into the bathroom she coughed until there was blood. Emily knew that it might be serious but said nothing. Doci tried to pretend that nothing was wrong.

The radiologist who read Doci's images had been on trauma call when Officer Marta Fuentes was brought into the Emergency Room. He remembered the exact point of lung and vessel penetration that the bullet took as it severed her life away.   He remembered looking at the angiogram from the operating room and saying that it wasn't survivable. He was right. And now, reviewing Doci's images he was surprised to see that she had grown a cancer in the exact same spot that the bullet lodged in Marta's lung. How could it be, he asked himself. Was the grandmother so tied in with her beloved that she would suffer the same fate only if only in a different way? He knew that Doci's tumor was inoperable. He was surprised to see from all earlier films that Doci's cancer had only developed since Marta's death. He had seen it before, somewhere in the interface between medicine and the forces that bind us. He knew that there is a connection, a truth that cannot be denied. He picked up his microphone and dictated the results.

The doctors brought Doci, Emily, and Snow into a room to discuss the options. Emily was touched that Doci introduced them both as her family, and that she would defer to them in all decision making. She seemed unusually calm. On the ride home her fate was not discussed, and not knowing how to react both Emily and Snow were quiet. At home Doci made some bread and cooked pasta with her homemade sauce that they all loved. She canned the tomatoes that she had picked from her garden on a prior August day. They even drank a little wine. Afterwards she told them a story about when she was young and in love. Afterwards Emily went upstairs and cried. Snow took a walk outside. Later in the evening Doci made them each a cup of hot cocoa and talked until their spirits had improved.

That night Snow and Emily held each other together in the bed like children. Neither was ready to lose the only person who had been able to put them on a path to healing. How could such a little lady, elderly, frail, and now dying have made such a difference for them they wondered. Finally when the last cloud covered the moon, their bellies full of chocolate and red wine, they drifted off into sleep heavy with the prospect of the loss of their rudder. Far from shore and still in choppy seas storms threatened. Storms had always threatened, but for the time Doci had entered the lives of

Emily and Snow, there was a certainty that they would be manageable. Now, neither could contemplate what the future would hold.

Doci died on a thursday at home. She had been in the hospital briefly to treat a painful bone metastasis, but she pleaded to be discharged. Emily and Snow were at her side, crying and lost. She had a half smile on her face. Even in death she had a generous look with kind and caring eyes.

Chapter 82

Three days after Doci died Emily was back in the alley with a needle in her arm. If she were a house her foundation had been washed away. All the progress that she had made with Doci's help was slipping. Recovery was made up the stairs, one step at a time, and relapse was down the elevator. It wasn't an unusually cold day in Erie but Emily felt the chill in her bones. She could go into the shelter she told herself, but that would be the last thing she would do. Somehow she needed to hold her ground in the alley she thought, if only symbolically it might be a small victory.

In a brief moment when the fear subsided and clarity ensued she thought about the fifteen million that she inherited, most of it in the bank, and in safe stocks and bonds that were paying good dividends. She could go to McDonald's if she wanted and get a cup of coffee, or even a cheeseburger. She didn't smell bad like before. They might even let her sit inside. No, she told herself. She would fight the urge to go to McDonald's. She wished for a minute that Doci would come to the alley all hunched over and gentle, and bring her a homemade ham sandwich and a diet Coke. She smiled for a moment and then truth returned. Doci wasn't coming back.

Emily Verada was back to being a homeless drug addict and occasional prostitute.

She could return to Doci's house, of course. She could stay there for as long as she wanted. Doci had told her that she was leaving everything to her that day in the hospital, that she was her only living relative. But she didn't need another inheritance. And she tried staying at the house. It just wasn't the same without Doci. The panic attacks returned. The flashbacks returned. She didn't feel safe there anymore.

Doci had said a lot that time in the hospital. It had happened so fast and Emily had been so upset she hadn't been able to digest it all. It was really the last conversation that the the two had had. After she was discharged the pain medication was strong and she slept a lot. She seemed to be listening and she gripped Emily's hand and squeezed it as if she heard when Emily told her how much she had helped her and how much she loved her and how much she wished she could live. But she didn't say anything. No, that all happened the last day that Emily visited her in the hospital.

Emily Verada's bottom was sore and cold. She was sitting on a patch of ice that was muddy. She was drifting from wakefulness to near slumber and was aroused slightly when the wind howled. She must have been thinking about the visit to the hospital because it kept coming back into her stream of thought. She didn't like hospitals. They frightened her. She was frightened on the day she visited Doci. They led her back to a dimly lit room and Doci was pale, but smiling. There were blue and yellow bruises on her arms from the frequent blood tests.   The gears of the intravenous were cycling. Some kind of therapy was entering her veins.

"Oh, Emily.   I am so happy you are here.   Where's Snow?"

"He's downstairs.   He's trying to get the courage to come up to see you."

"Oh sweetheart, tell him I want him to come up. You know I think you make a wonderful couple. Both of you are so attractive. I feel lucky to have you both in my life."

Emily didn't say anything even in recollection.   She might have smiled, but she didn't remember. Doci continued.

"You know Emily, whatever happens to me I will always be watching over you. You are the most important person in the entire world as far as I am concerned and I only see good things for you."

"Yeah, but..." Emily stopped.

Doci looked at her and encouraged. "I know. It is tough to see to the destination when your boat is passing a storm at sea. But I know you will make it."

Emily was quiet again, even in recollection, but she heard Doci's words more clearly now, after the fact.   Doci continued, but was tiring and spoke softly.

"You know Emily Snow has a plan to get to the man who tortured you and killed Marta."

"I know. He told me." Emily was dismissive. She knew how cruel Murtins was.   And she knew that the best of law enforcement was working on the case.   She didn't believe there was any real prospect of bringing him to justice, at last not on her own. Doci continued.

"When I lost Marta my life was shattered. Soon I will be reunited with her which is good."

Emily said nothing but listened. Doci had Emily's hand in her own and she gripped it tightly. Emily let her finish.

"And when I heard what Mr. Murtins had done to you and the others it reminded me of something that happened to me when I was a young girl."

Emily looked up as Doci continued.

"I had the opportunity to retaliate and I didn't"

Emily looked at her in the dim light. She appeared quite serious. "Of course you didn't. You don't have a vengeful bone in your body."

Doci continued unchallenged. There were noises from other patients on the floor and a siren whaled in the distance.

"Emily, I regret that I didn't. I do."

Emily was surprised. She said nothing. She squeezed Doci's hand and Doci did not squeeze back. Doci smiled a half smile, as if she had made a confession. A confession for a crime that she had contemplated but did not commit.

Outside the sky had become very dark. Emily told herself that she didn't believe in revenge. She told herself that Doci didn't believe in it either. Doci's talk must have been the effect of a medication, she told herself. She went downstairs and convinced Snow to visit Doci briefly, but when the two went back she was deeply asleep.

In the alley the wind whistled and the icy patch where Emily rested did not offer any comfort. A few stragglers dipped their heads into the alcove but Emily rested in the darkest shadows and was not visible to them. They looked for a moment and moved on, maybe to the shelter, or to their own place of momentary peace. Emily didn't think about Doci's words again. She didn't have to. They were already inside of her and powerfully gaining a life of their own.

Chapter 83

The conversation that Emily wanted to have with Doci was about her son. She wanted to tell Doci that getting him back was the most important thing to her and that she wanted any advice that Doci could give. Unfortunately, like many conversations intended but never conveyed the words were not spoken. As Emily drifted off to sleep in the dark part of the alley she dreamed of Doci, pale and waxy, but alert and understanding. She took her hand and spoke.

"Doci, I love you. Thank you so much for everything you have done. You have helped me immeasurably."

"And what is it you want next, Emily?"

"Of course I want to continue to get well, and maybe run again, or go back to school."

"Is that all?"

"No. Most importantly I want to have my son back. I want us to be a family."

"With Snow?"

"Yes, of course."

Doci looked at Emily carefully in the dim light. Her eyes were slightly gray and sunken, but they were alert. Her shoulders were relaxed and her appearance, even under her present circumstances, was reassuring. She waited before she spoke and then did so in a whisper. There was a slight rattle which came from her chest as she breathed. Emily moved closer to listen carefully.

"Three Blue Candles, Emily. Three Blue Candles."

Since it was only a dream Emily could not respond. She could only smile slightly as she drifted into a deeper sleep. She was ill equipped for the night with the cold and the wind. The soiled blanket that she had used in the past was gone. She had no food nor drink. The cardboard box that she had used for ground cover and wind abatement had been taken. And the one person who had helped her most was now dead. The moon had moved behind a cloud and it felt unusually dark in the alley that night. All of these things weighed on Emily's half slumbering consciousness. Nevertheless she felt a small ray of hope circling somewhere nearby.

Chapter 84

After four days in the cold Emily moved into the shelter. She hated it there and resisted going but in the end she saw it as her only option. Her plan was to defrost for a day or so and then return to the alley. Normally the shelter wouldn't take her in until after 4 p.m. but when the social worker looked at her condition she was promptly brought upstairs. It wasn't an hour later when she had her first visitor. The young woman was brought to the sleeping Emily and had to look for a minute before she could recognize her. She was surprised how disheveled Emily appeared, and the stench of urine made her keep her distance.

"No. Please don't wake her. I can come back."

Emily opened her eyes. It was Nicki. She smiled. Despite the barriers the two hugged tightly.

"I'm back in town to get started at Mary Herman. They are letting me start mid semester."

Emily said nothing. She was trying to get oriented. They looked at each other and Emily started to explain. Before she could talk Nicki interjected.

"Thanks to you, Emily."

After a long pause Emily spoke.

"Doci died."

Nicki looked at her. "Yes I know. That's partly why I am here."

"Oh."

"They called me looking for you. I tried the Sewickley number and Doci's place. I tried the city mission and the shelter everyday, and I even went looking for the alley."

Emily was silent. She felt slightly embarrassed by her disheveled state. Nicki continued.

"It's Snow. Apparently he unravelled after Doci died and he went back to drinking. That led to a fight in the bar and he was arrested."

Emily looked at Nicki surprised. She continued.

"I guess he had no money for bail, so as far as I know he is still at the City Jail."

Emily looked up. "We need to get him out of there. Can we use your car?"

"Of course. Do you want to take a shower?"

"Yeah, I better. Maybe I can call my mom's attorney. Can you wait here for a few minutes?"

"Sure, Emily."

Emily was animated. Snow was in some kind of trouble and needed her help. How could she be so selfish she told herself. He was going through a difficult time as well.

Outside the afternoon sun had surfaced and the icicles were dripping everywhere. The wind was still and the traffic flowed with a daytime urgency. Nicki and Emily were together again and they were working to get Snow's release. For a moment Emily was not thinking about her own troubles. She had other fish to fry.

Chapter 85

Nicki and Emily sat in a brightly light room with shiny walls.   Across from them through a wire-imbedded glass partition Snow held his head in his hands. He wore an orange jump suit and had a white cast on his right arm.   When he looked up he revealed a right sided raccoon eye.   His countenance was a mix between embarrassment and good fortune. He was happy to see Emily.   He remembered Nicki from their recent trip to Harrisburg.   He spoke through a telephone handset.

"Thanks for coming Emily?"

Emily was unkempt. Her hair was matted and her jacket soiled.   But she smiled and was happy to see Snow.   She wondered what had happened. She presumed drinking, then a fight, maybe over his prosthesis. Snow was slow to anger but had a furious temper. She spoke quietly.

"I missed you."

Snow took in a deep breath. He acknowledged Nicki and sat back in his chair. A guard stood nearby on Snow's side pretending not to eavesdrop. Snow spoke quickly as if had gained an insight.

"Before Iraq when I played football I had lots of friends. Girls would call me and want to get together. Things were always looking up. But then I went over there and lost those men and everything changed. My friends are gone. The people that had promised to help have left, and no girls are calling me now."

Emily waited until the bright room had become quiet. Even the guard felt anxious with the pause. Then she spoke.

"I'll call you."

Snow looked up. "You will?"

"Sure, Snow. But we've got to get you out of here first."

Nicki smiled. Snow smiled. The guard even held back a smile. Emily continued. "I think losing Doci hit you pretty hard. I am going to call my mom's attorney and find out what we have to do. Nicki and I will be back as soon as we get things sorted out. Don't get too down on your self. You are a good man, Snow."

Snow looked up in relief. He was fighting back a small tear that had formed in his right eye. He covered it with his hand and spoke.

"Thanks Emily. I appreciate it."

Emily nodded and and she and Nicki left through a door that had to be buzzed open from a distance. The two worked from Doci's house making calls and faxing information. Nicki agreed to stay over for a few days. With Nicki there Emily felt comfortable taking a shower and washing some things. Later when they ordered out for pizza they had some laughs and Emily briefly had a feeling just like old times. When that feeling came it made her giddy and then it scared her. She wondered when the next shoe would drop. But that evening warm in her bed with her tummy full and Nicki beside her she felt a particular calm. She even whispered gratitude for having Snow in her life.

Chapter 86

That night the dreams that Emily experienced were particularly vivid. She tossed in her bed and had some awareness of dreaming but even Snow became disturbed and tried to wake her.

"Emily, you are shouting in your sleep. You are going to wake Nicki downstairs."

Emily responded from the place between dream and deep sleep.

"Yeah, Ok. Sorry."

She found herself in a gingerbread house. It wasn't friendly however. The house was tilting and the cake had become too hard to eat. Doci and Pa were upstairs eating with her mom and dad. Some of the girls that Murtins had killed were in the attic trying on a shipment of new clothes. Snow was outside and trying to force the door to open. It would not budge. His key would not work. He was visibly upset. He began knocking at the window and shouting for Emily to come outside. She could not hear him. Nicki was at the backdoor and was trying frantically to ring the bell. Outside there was an area where the ice had frozen and Emily's sister was skating. She had become a very accomplished skater and was showing off. But that ice was thin she told herself. If it cracks she might fall through.

On the main floor of the gingerbread house Emily held a sword. Across from her sitting in a high backed chair Fred Murtins removed his sword from its sheath and began polishing it. He seemed unusually calm and confident. Emily spoke nervously.

"Evil and its agents must be slain. Are you who you say you are?"

Murtins looked at her. He had the look that burned into Emily's soul. He spoke with confidence.

"It is me."

Emily said nothing. Murtins continued.

"You cannot harm me with your sword. It is flimsy and dull."

Emily studied him nervously. In her bed she was dripping with sweat and her heart pounded. Murtins smiled and continued.

"Even if you somehow prevail I know you will put me in your basement so you can be reminded that I am slain."

Emily responded with a forceful voice. "When you are slain I will decide were you will lie."

"If I am in your basement I will remain in your house. I will remain your tormenter."

Emily thought for a minute and studied her weapon. Then she spoke. "If you are slain you will be banished from this house. I guarantee you that, you evil bastard."

Murtins laughed and chewed on a piece of the gingerbread wall. Emily stood and presented her sword. Murtins counseled.

"Emily, you are not capable of revenge. I know that for a fact. You are burdened by conscience, by justice, and by your moral beliefs. You may be angry but you will not be able to fight when our swords clash."

Emily sat up in her bed and thrashed her imaginary sword violently and screamed.

"I can fight! I can fight! And I will fight! You will see what I can and can't do!"

Murtins took another piece of the gingerbread and chewed on it. He appeared totally unconcerned with Emily's threat. His calm demeanor unnerved her. Snow was now awakened and was gently tapping Emily but she would not come out of what had become a seizure. There was a time early in her recovery when Emily had powerful dreams and had wet the bed. Now, a prisoner of catharsis, the entire bed was wet. Emily was grunting loudly. She had passed a tipping point. She could not be stopped. Snow was frightened. He went quickly to get Nicki from downstairs.

Murtins stood and pointed his sword Emily's way. She felt his rage. He was coming toward her. He wanted to extinguish her once and for all. Emily stood nervously and prepared to fight. Then at the top of the stairs she saw Doci who held the railing and spoke out.

"Emily, dear. I am upstairs. If you need me I will come down and help you sweetheart. You have nothing to worry about, dear. I will be here if you need me. Just let me know what you need."

Emily was gasping for air. The sheets had been thrown across the room.   Her chest rose and fell like a straining bellows.   The mattress was drenched with urine and sweat. Nicki and Snow were standing in the corner of the room watching. Emily looked transformed. She was awake now. She looked up at the others and smiled a like a cat.

Chapter 87

The sign on the door read "Department of Public Welfare, Child and Youth Protective Services". Emily was dressed in a grey suit. She sat next to her attorney, Liz, who had once been her mom's golfing partner and had worked for a time to have Emily declared incompetent in her inheritance case. That was forgotten now, although Liz felt a special need to treat Emily well, and Emily believed that worked in her favor. Emily and Liz were petitioning the agency for the return of her son, now fourteen months old. Before cases like this could proceed to any serious litigation they had to be heard by a panel of social and case workers who would make a recommendation to a judge.

Three panel members sat across the table from Emily and asked questions from messy piles of folders and notes. Snow and Nicki sat in the corner away from the table and were prepared to speak as character witnesses, if necessary. Liz was optimistic. Emily owned two homes, one in Sewickley and one in Millcreek. She was financially well off even after the recent stock market tumble. She was in a committed relationship. There had been a few minors scuffles with the law that related to her homelessness and drug use, but nothing in the last six months. Liz was certain that they would convince the panel that Emily was both a fit mother and had the resources to provide for her child.   It seemed a "no brainer".

Even though the questions were routine the panel struggled to get through them.   They were cheerful enough but they focused on Emily's illness, her prior drug use and prostitution, and her withdrawal from Mary Herman College. Liz objected to their questioning but tried to be deferential. After the panel was finished they asked the petitioners to wait outside in an ante-room.   Emily, Liz, Snow and Nicki sat in a waiting room for what seemed like a long time while the panel conferred.   After some time the door opened and everyone was invited back in. There was nervous laughter and small talk and then the panel informed the child's mother that they would make a recommendation for a judge's review and that he would contact her through the mail. Despite Liz's counsel that this was not a bad outcome Emily felt dejected. She said nothing on the drive back to Millcreek and went to bed without eating dinner.

If Emily and the others could have been in the room where the panel met they would have learned that the toddler had been named Becker and was adored by the foster mom. She would have learned that he was healthy, active, strong, and curious.   They would have learned that panel members such as themselves were appointed by the city counsel and one of the candidates for office had expressed an interest in adopting this beautiful boy. All of this information would later be discovered by Liz and her team from Pittsburgh but for now

Emily only knew that she had an ache in her chest that would not heal. She felt it everyday. It did not leave her.

Chapter 88

Snow and Emily had rehearsed it many times. They rehearsed around contingencies. The rehearsed what they would do in almost any scenario. Nicki had played the role of the others. She had tried to thwart them, but at least in the rehearsals, she was not able to push them off plan. The uniforms had arrived. They had researched and created the documents. They had meticulously researched and tested the Radio Frequency and GPS imbedded devices. They had obtained the audio surveillance transmitters. They were ready.

On the morning of "Day One", as they called it, Nicki, Snow and Emily drove and parked the yellow beetle down the street from the halfway house where Fred Murtin's wife lived. Her location was easy enough to find. In this regard they turned to Bob LeClair who immediately provided the information from the database that he had built. He further shared the transcripts of interviews and depositions that she had given over the prior year. Apparently she was not being detained technically, but had entered into an agreement to live at sort of a safe house and wear an ankle bracelet. Her son was placed in foster care. Up to this point Ms. Murtins had not provided any credible clues to Fred Murtin's whereabouts.

Bob LeClair wondered out loud if she actually knew where he was.

Snow and Nicki knocked on the door of the facility. They were greeted by someone who appeared to be the house mother. Emily spoke. "We have an urgent message for Mrs. Fred Murtins. We are here on behalf of the Ukrainian Consulate."

The house mother smiled. "Really?"

Snow and Emily tried to stay in role. Their acting now had the feel of a college prank. They were led into a common room with couches and a few computer desks. A number of women populated the common room. Emily scanned their faces and guessed that they had been battered or abused. Some looked at Snow nervously. The house mother spoke.

"Can you wait here? I will get her?"

Snow and Emily nodded and stood at attention. Emily carried a large briefcase which held the papers that they had prepared. After a time Snow broke off and planted some listening devices near the community phone and in the hallway. By now the women in the common room seemed uninterested. After some time a quite heavy woman walked slowly out with a walker. She was short of breath. Emily immediately noticed her large, swollen legs and the large bracelet that wrapped around the right ankle.

Emily began. "Mrs. Murtins?"

"Yes." She answered nervously. She had been through a tough year herself, not the perpetrator of any crime, but convicted by association. She had lost her son and had been condemned to a life of constant monitoring. Her health had failed and she was penniless. She wondered what was next.

Emily continued. "We have travelled from the Ukrainian Embassy in Buffalo, New York. May we talk with you in private?"

Mrs. Murtins paused and then nodded. She led them down a dimly lit hallway and then into a small room with a table, chair, and hospital bed. Emily had not pictured the wife of her attacker to look or act like this. She felt a pang of sympathy for her. She stayed in role, however. While Emily spoke Snow reached behind his back and placed a listening device under the table and on the wall behind the chair. Emily continued.

"Mrs. Murtins, your husband has been named the sole beneficiary in the recent death of one his Ukrainian relatives. The firm who represents the estate has retained us to see that he has an opportunity to claim his inheritance."

Murtins paused. "So I am not in any further trouble?"

"No Ma'am, but we need your help in locating your husband."

Murtins looked up. "I have no idea where he is?" She looked about reflexively and continued. "How much did he inherit?"

Emily had anticipated the question. "According to the documents that we have he will own two homes, land, and a moderate sum of cash."

Murtins showed interest. "Cash?"

Emily continued. "Yes. By today's exchange the cash is valued at over $190,000 United States dollars."

Murtins smiled. Emily continued.

"And the homes and land can be sold for additional dollars, if Mr. Murtins agrees."

Murtins was now sitting on the edge of the bed. She was smiling. "I can accept the money for him. I will see that he gets it."

Emily corrected. "Ma'am, we are only able to release the settlement directly to him. He can sign these papers in the presence of consular staff, or he can visit us directly in Buffalo or New York City."

Murtins looked puzzled. Snow could see the conflict that was brewing inside her. Now as they had rehearsed both were silent. Absolute silence. They did not say a word. Murtins looked at them for guidance. Silence. After a long time she blurted out.

"Give me the papers. I don't know my husband's location but I may be able to locate someone who can find him. $190,000 U.S. dollars, right."

Neither Snow nor Emily smiled. They had rehearsed this moment with Nicki. After a long pause Emily handed Murtins the papers and spoke in a matter of fact tone.

"Ma'am, here are the documents he needs to sign. Time is of the essence. I believe he needs to sign them within ten days in the presence of a consular representative or he may forfeit some of his rights. Did you have any other questions?"

Murtins looked at the two emissaries. "No, thank you. I will be certain that he gets them."

Ms. Murtins tried to get up from the bed. She was holding the folder that Emily had given her. Snow was already in the hall now. He spoke for the first time.

"That's alright. You don't have to get up. We can find our way out."

Emily and Snow walked professionally for two blocks before they turned the corner, looked both ways and then gave each other a "high five". The sun had come out from behind a large cloud and was warming their backs as they leaned on the car and updated Nicki through the open window. Within a few minute Snow had the listening devices up and broadcasting. They had tagged the documents mailer with a GPS sending device and soon would be monitoring position and location on their laptop. Either Mrs. Murtins would call her husband, or his "go between" or she would mail the folder. Either way they would be closer to what they called "day two".

Chapter 89

Snow and Emily followed a red dot on a map as the folio tracked across the country.   First in New Stanton, Pennsylvania, then eastward to West Hartford, Connecticut. They tracked the items in real time on Snow's laptop as Emily drove first Interstate 80 and then to the north and east. It sat in East Hartford for a night and then proceeded to New Haven. Then it moved slowly across the city and rested at the Tweedy Smythe Airport for two days. After a seeming eternity in the parking lot the dot moved at foot speed to an isolated area of a building, appeared to be transferred, and then left the facility through an employee lot, first slowly then at car speed. Snow and Emily were tired, but relieved. They fully expected their signal would take flight and exit beyond their ability to quickly follow.   They followed the signal to a residential neighborhood in West Reading and zeroed in on an older, white, cape cod style home in need of repair.   There was no name on the mailbox and the curtains were pulled shut. Emily felt her heart race. She knew he was near. They parked on a side street out of view and Emily walked to the house.

The air was calm.   Three crows sat on the roof of the house. They were motionless, waiting. A chipmunk stood frozen on the steel railing that skirted the cement porch. In the next yard a cat turned and was completely quiet. The cat studied Emily. The bright sun moved behind a cloud and the cloud fixed its position in the afternoon sky. Emily knocked at the door. First nothing then someone coming.

In the avalanche of time between her knocking and the door opening Emily said the prayer that she had rehearsed again and again. "Please God forgive me for what I am about to do. You can punish me as you see fit after I am finished but now I ask you to give me the strength to complete my task at hand. Thank you God."

The door opened. She saw the eye. It was him. Inside there was pushing and scratching. Words were exchanged. Snow could hear yelling and he moved up to the window behind the bush. He would go in if Emily needed him, but now it was her time. She needed to finish the job she started. He knew that she would. Emily had a poisoned dart. It only grazed his neck and he pulled it from the wall and threw it back at her. She took out her knife and stabbed him in the neck and in the leg. They were on the floor and he crawled to the corner to get his bat. He raised up and took a swing at her with great force but he missed and she caught the shaft of it on the follow through and wrestled it away from him. He was feeling the effects of the poison and the stab wounds in his neck but he still had fight in him. Oddly, Emily looked across the room and saw what she thought were Officer Marta Fuentes and Julie LeClair sitting in arm chairs. At first they were signaling encouragement but when she glanced back they were gone. She raised up the bat and struck him across the head. He lay quietly on the floor.

Emily studied Fred Murtins briefly before she dragged him to the bedroom as she had planned. Snow was pouring the lighter fluid around the outside of the house and Emily had taken out fishing line and a large needle as she had planned. Murtins lay naked and unconscious on the bed. When she finished her work she exited through the living room, a match was lit and they made their way back to the car. As they slowly left West Reading they heard the screeching of fire engines and police vehicles. Inside their car things were quiet.

Chapter 90

From the top of East Rock Emily and Snow could see the town of New Haven and its magnificent university buildings. To the south and west was the harbor and further to the west they saw the black smoke rising and forming a grey cloud. It was a nearly windless day and the dark cloud seemed to sit alone in the sky of the late afternoon. Emily felt lighter. She sat on a bench near the edge of the cliff and held Snow's hand.

"You know I haven't been running in a long time. Maybe I could try running again. What do you think?"

Snow looked at her in the afternoon sunlight. He spoke encouragingly. "You know I think there is a mountain bike in the garage in our Millcreek home. Maybe I could ride along with you."

"That would be great, Snow. Do you think you could ride it?"

Snow looked at her and smiled. "I could try."

By now he had his arm around her. The air was quite pleasant. Emily encouraged back. "That's the spirit."

The two sat at the top of East Rock park and studied the horizon for nearly an hour. Neither was in a hurry to leave. Down below and closer to the crime scene Bob LeClair sat in a lawn chair and watched the Murtin's house burn out of control. He had been monitoring Emily and Snow's position since they had last been in communication. And when he had a sense they were moving in he got quickly on their heels. He watched the fire and police do their jobs and he watched the paramedics take Fred Murtins from the burning house but he couldn't assess his condition. Later, when he took a long walk through the neighborhood near the burned house he tried to assemble his feelings but could not. He only knew it had become dark and cold and he told himself it was time to move on.

Chapter 91

The West Reading Police Department dispatched detectives to the burning house and to the hospital. Later the group met over some coffee and bagels. They were a group not fazed by violent crime. On their beat and with the current economy violent crime was a regular occurrence. Unspoken, but believed, violent crime was job security. And in an odd way that was a good thing. The tallest of the four scratched his silver mustache and led the briefing.

"It appeared to be a simple house fire but after they took him out it was clear this was the murder-arson deal."

Two of the others were rotund and wore white shirts and ties. They perspired even on a cold days. The younger one spoke. "Yeah, whoever had it in for this guy was sending a message. Apparently his privates were sewn to the bed with fishing line. He got quite a wound when they pulled him out of there."

There was chuckling. The fourth detective with the shaved head chimed in. "That will put a crimp on your weekend."

"Yes, you are right." The tall man conceded. "Who went to the hospital?"

"The youngest of the group answered. "I did, sir. But they took him to surgery."

"Did he say anything?"

"Yes, sir."

"What did it say?"

The young detective opened his note file and looked it over. Then he spoke. "Something about the number 23. That this was the end for the number 23. Something like that."

The others shook their heads. That probably won't be helpful they thought. More coffee was poured. The first detective finished.

"How is he doing?"

He is pretty beat up. He's got some burns, and his privates are pretty torn up. But I think he will probably survive."

The leader sipped on his coffee and continued his questioning. "Why are the Feds involved?"

One of the rotund detectives answered. "This guy works over at the airport, TSA I think. I guess because he is a federal agent or something."

The leader looked around. There was nothing else to discuss. He assigned the case. They would have another briefing in the morning.

Chapter 92

The following day Bob LeClair drove to Princeton, New Jersey and parked in the grassy area behind the field house. He hadn't planned the trip but was surprised to see that the women's varsity tennis team was playing a match with the bulldogs of Yale. The match was in progress when Bob took a seat alone in the stands. The fans were deferential but the contest had come down to one set between the final two competitors. Bob sat alone in the wooden bleachers. The Princeton player was behind in the third set four to one. She was serving. At a particularly quiet moment Bob yelled loudly to the competitor.

"Go Tigers. You can do it. Go Julie. Show her some heat!"

If there was embarrassment Bob did not recognize it. If it was a lapse of name Bob didn't notice it. But if it had been Julie, as he had dreamed, today she would have fought back and won, if only for her dad. The competitor held serve and received at four games to two. Bob's cheering continued. Rather than scold with their eyes some of the other fans began to catch Bob's enthusiasm and join in the boisterous support. The competitor broke her opponents serve, held her own and tied the match at four games to four. By now Bob had moved closer to court level. When Julie was alive he had watched endless matches and knew that momentum could turn on a dime. It appeared that in the late day sun Princeton was making a run. When the final score was posted the last match had turned the tide in favor of the Tigers. Bob felt proud of his team and their effort. It was a team he did not know. It was his first visit to the campus.

Later, after the participants congratulated each other for fine play and the players gathered their things the final competitor approached Bob from across the fence.

"Hey Mister. I appreciate your support, thanks."

Bob was touched. He struggled to respond in kind. "Nice comeback. You were great to watch."

The young competitor continued. "My name is Nancy. I hope we see you out here again. Take Care."

Bob replied. "I'll do my best. Good Luck, Nancy."

That evening Bob LeClair made the long drive home to Ohio. He played the radio and tapped his fingers to the music. It was the first time that he had played the radio in his truck since his daughter had died. He didn't feel any different. He just wanted to listen to some music. He was thankful that he had seen the college athletes play that day. It was a great match to watch even though he only saw the ending. Next time he would show up for the entire thing. She did play tough and she fought hard he told himself. It was good to see her come back and win.

www.ingramcontent.com/pod-product-compliance
Lightning Source LLC
Chambersburg PA
CBHW051549250626
47157CB00001B/235